As True As I'm Sittin' Here

"As True As I'm Sittin' Here"

200 CAPE BRETON STORIES

COLLECTED BY ARCHIE NEIL CHISHOLM

EDITED BY

BRIAN SUTCLIFFE AND RONALD CAPLAN

WITH FOLKLORE MOTIFS BY MICHAEL TAFT

Breton Books

Editor: Ronald Caplan

Production Assistance: Bonnie Thompson
with Ray Martheleur and James Fader (Artplus)

Transcription: Brian Sutcliffe

Cover Photographs: Ronald Caplan

We acknowledge the support of
the Canada Council for the Arts for our publishing program.

We also acknowledge support from Cultural Affairs,
Nova Scotia Department of Tourism and Culture.

Canadian Cataloguing in Publication Data

Main entry under title:

As true as I'm sittin' here

ISBN 1-895415-58-6

1. Tales — Nova Scotia — Cape Breton Island. I. Caplan, Ronald, 1942-
II. Title: Archie Neil's Cape Breton (Radio program).

GR113.5.C36A7 2000 398.2'09716'9 C00-950143-6

Contents

201 Stories: An Introduction

The last 20 years have made an awful dent in Cape Breton storytelling. While more storytellers have come along, I dwell on the older ones, those who can never be replaced. They coloured our air—wildly, delightfully—and, I wish, indelibly. They shortened the road, lightened our work, filled the pauses between tunes. Their stories are the comebacks and one-ups, barbs and jokes, wonder tales and just what-we-make-of-what-you-might-otherwise-call "ordinary daily life." They are those marvelous ways of cutting us down while uplifting our hearts.

But nothing is so ephemeral as a good story. And it is in this light that I am particularly grateful to offer the 200 stories in *As True As I'm Sittin' Here*. They were collected for a rare CBC radio show called "Archie Neil's Cape Breton."

Archie Neil Chisholm was himself irreplaceable. Taken, faults and all, he was a Cape Breton saint. A fiddler, storyteller and much-sought-after master of ceremonies for Cape Breton concerts, he was host of the radio show. Much of the show's music was live, in the studio—and it helped open doors for The Barra MacNeils, Rita MacNeil, The Rankin Family, fiddler Jerry Holland and many more. It also saved the 200 stories in this book.

Working with producer Brian Sutcliffe and station manager Burt Wilson, Archie Neil left the studio to collect stories in some of the settings where good stories are born and thrive—kitchens and living rooms throughout Cape Breton Island. Given the right atmosphere, the storytellers teased and bickered, inspired laughter and chills, and reminded of events kept alive only by these tales. And the Canadian Broadcasting Corporation recorded it all.

"Archie Neil's Cape Breton" was on air for just three seasons. After that, for a couple of summers, the stories were used as fillers, a series called "As True As I'm Sittin' Here."

Then it was over. Until now.

ACTUALLY, THERE ARE OVER 200 STORIES in this book, and one of them is told below by Tommy Peggy MacDonald. I add it here as an excuse to use Tommy Peggy's photograph on the front cover. Tommy Peggy never told a story on "Archie Neil's Cape Breton," although his voice was heard there as one of the North Shore Gaelic Singers. On the other hand, Tommy Peggy was one of our loveliest storytellers, and one of the first people to tell me stories when I came to Cape Breton. He was one of those people who knew how to rein in the moment until it trotted at his own particular pace, his voice gentle and assured and with a little bit of laughter at the back of each breath. Years ago, sitting under an overturned rowboat at Little River harbour, while rain drizzled around us, he sat mending a mackerel net and told me the following story about a Reiteach.

Now, Reiteach (pronounced "ray-tchuck") is a Gaelic word for making a clearing, as in cutting away small spruce, preparing the ground. It was used to mean a very formal way of asking a father for his daughter's hand in marriage. As Tommy Peggy explained, men would go to the house one evening, perhaps take a bottle along, and the girl likely would not have much say one way or another. The father would decide. He told it first in Gaelic and then in English. Here's how Tommy Peggy's story went:

"In a lot of cases, it might be the first time the groom had ever seen the prospective wife—and in a lot of instances it wasn't a very happy episode for the girl, but it turned out quite happily after that for most of them. I know of one particular case—I wasn't there but I knew the people involved—it happened the girl had never seen the man brought before her this particular night for the Reiteach. This man had got the marriage garb to marry another woman, and she had jilted him. It was the custom then the man bought the apparel for his wife to be married in along with his own. I don't know whether this woman returned the clothes or did she get married in it to another fellow. Anyway, she jilted this man.

"But the young fellows wanted to have the wedding, by hook or by crook. There was one fellow just full of devilment. They were fishing, and they used to have shacks down at the shore—fish, and stay there all night—and this one night they were trying to figure out how they were going to get a wedding. This man said they'd take the man to his sister.

"They got a bottle or two of whiskey, I don't know how many of them went. I doubt the girl had ever seen the man because he was quite a bit older, and she lived six miles away. But the idea there was he was more or less a little more prominent citizen of the community and the parents were quite willing to look at the matter in that light. The girl was taken by surprise and she cried her heart out that night.

"But I heard of her relating the story years after to the women at a carding and spinning frolic, and she said in the final analysis—she was talking in Gaelic, of course—after all the discontent of that first night, they had eight children together, and she said, 'Do you know that I never let one of them sleep one night between my husband and myself.'"

Tommy Peggy finished the story. I suppose the rain had stopped. Happily, my tape recorder was still running. And I left there knowing I had a good story for *Cape Breton's Magazine*, something to pass over to the wider world. And I pass it over to you, here.

I LOVE THESE KINDS OF STORIES. They are the salt and pepper of any Cape Breton meal. There are over 200 stories here—and that's not the end of them. Barely the beginning. Right now, out there somewhere, folks are proudly making more. Every time the cloud crosses the moon, every time a mouse moves a blade of grass, every time a politician opens his mouth—like a bear trap or a camera, you can count on one of these antennae of the race picking it up and responding with comments. The ghosts are seen. And we can at least take comfort in our wits.

Ronald Caplan
Wreck Cove

ACKNOWLEDGEMENTS: The Type and Motif numbers at the end of each story, and in the index starting on page 203, were provided by folklorist Michael Taft, using Aarne and Thompson's *The Types of the Folk Tale* and Stith Thompson's *Motif-Index of Folk Literature.* This is a scholarly way of showing that these stories, so intimately rooted in this place, are also part of the folk literature of the whole wide world.

This book does not contain *all* the stories collected for "Archie Neil's Cape Breton"—but over 200 is a pretty good start! And I want to thank all those families and friends who helped us search for and, usually, locate the storytellers. Special thanks go to Cecelia Cooke—an unsung archivist with vital knowledge of the history of Cape Breton's CBC—and to Greg Smith, Paddy and Marie (MacLellan) MacDonald, Mr. and Mrs. John Dan MacIsaac, Jackie MacNeil, Margaret (Archie Neil) Chisholm, Jim St. Clair, Mary and Frank MacInnis, Buddy (T. R.) MacDonald, Jackie MacInnis, and Doug MacPhee. The search continues, and we welcome any additional information.

As True As I'm Sittin' Here

JIM ST. CLAIR

MULL RIVER

1.

A woman went from Sporting Mountain to North Sydney when the train first went through Orangedale. She went down to see a doctor. And the train had only been going along the track for, maybe, six or eight months.

She went down on the morning train and she had an appointment with this doctor in North Sydney. Since trains ran with great frequency in those days she was able, in the afternoon, to get a train back to Sporting Mountain.

Oh, there were a lot of people travelling on the train. It was full of people going from the country into Sydney and North Sydney and from the Sydneys back out into the country. To Grand Narrows and Iona and all those places.

Anyhow, the woman saw the doctor and she found out what was wrong with her. He told her that she should take some medication.

Well, she got on the train and she said to the conductor, "Would you please tell me when we get to Orangedale?"

Now Orangedale would be about twenty-five miles nearer North Sydney than Sporting Mountain, where she was going to get off. Well, the conductor said, Yes, he could do that.

So, she sat back in the seat and she was watching the scenery go by and she was feeling a little better. She'd seen the doctor and everything was going to be better. Gradually, with the motion of the train, she fell asleep.

The train came to Orangedale and the luggage was unloaded and the freight was unloaded and they gave the signal to go ahead. Off went the train towards West Bay, near her home at Sporting Mountain.

They got about five miles down the track when the conductor realized that Mrs. MacPhail was still sitting there. She was kind of, just nodding. "Oh my goodness!" the conductor said. "That woman, she needed to know when we got to Orangedale!"

He went to the front of the car and pulled the emergency handle and the train came to a stop. The conductor went up to the engineer, three or four cars ahead, and he said, "We have to go back to Orangedale. I made a terrible mistake."

They put the train in reverse and they backed up the five miles and they came to Orangedale. The conductor went to Mrs. MacPhail and he kind of shook her and he said, "You wanted to know when we got to Orangedale. Can I help you off with your luggage?"

"Oh no," she said. "Just give me a glass of water. The doctor told me to take my pills in Orangedale and I'd be fine when I got home."

J1820. Inappropriate action from misunderstanding

2.

I was thinking on the way down about the witch of Mull River. She was born in the 1700s and she lived all the way through the 1800s and died in 1906, at the age of a hundred and eight. She was well known to have had the evil eye, all of her life.

She was born in Scotland and settled in Prince Edward Island, and then came to Mabou and then settled at Livingston's Mountain in Mull River, where she lived the rest of her life.

She had a very, very crooked tooth, and there was a man who

made fun of her crooked tooth. She fixed this evil eye on him and, from that day, for twenty years, his mouth was just wide open. He wasn't able to close it, so they say.

She was known to be able to make milk go across distances. She had the facility, somehow or other, when her own cows would be dry, of putting a pair of gloves on a willow rod. She'd point that willow rod in whatever direction the best cow was in the neighbourhood and there she would be, milking those gloves. There'd be no milk in the neighbour's cow but there'd be milk in her own creamer.

There was a Beaton family—they were from the Judique Beatons—the witch's only son went to work for them when he was quite young. They had no children of their own so they decided to turn him against his own mother. She got wind of this and she came down to where they lived. The woman came to the door and said, "Ah-ha, I know you're Dan's mother." And she picked a rotten cheese out of the press and she threw it on the dust and said to Mrs. Livingston, "There, that rotten cheese will pay for your son. Now go home."

The witch of Mull River fixed her evil eye on the woman and said, "Where that cheese lies in the dust, there will be grass growing but my family will go on forever while your house will fall."

And the fact of the matter is, that where that happened there is today no house. There's a field. Whereas the witch's family is still continuing.

And I think that, when she died, a cousin of my mother's was there. When she died, this old witch, she was sweeping the floor. She was hanging on to the broom and she simply died.

They put her in her bed and put her face to the wall, so that nobody could see her face, and every picture in the house and every mirror was turned so that there would be no image maintained of her.

Next to her broom, there was some kind of a leather sack which she had never let anyone look into. They took that and they threw it in the fireplace and the chimney of the house blew up.

And that was the end, as far as I know, of the witch of Mull River.

D2071. Evil eye

D2083.3. Milk transferred from another's cow by magic

3.

The smartest dog I ever heard about was an old, old dog. And these people lived in a large house that had two big roofs to it. In those days they'd have lots of ladders going from one roof to the next and from the ground to the first roof. It was a house built in two parts.

Well anyway, the old dog got pretty old and he didn't like to run. So the man of the house got a new dog to go after the cows. The man himself wasn't terribly, you know, enthusiastic about going looking for cows either.

So, this day, there was somebody there, and he said he couldn't believe how smart the old dog was. The man would whistle and the two dogs would come to him. The young dog would sit down on the ground and look up into the pasture. The old dog would climb, sort of arthritically, up the first ladder to the first roof. He'd look around to see if he could see the cows. Then he'd climb up the ladder to the second roof. The second roof was the one where the chimney of the house came out.

Well, the old dog would be pretty tired by the time he got up there. With one paw leaning on the chimney, to rest himself, with his second paw he'd shade his eyes from the sun and he'd look around up into the pasture to see where the cows were. When he'd see where the cows were, he'd take his paw and he'd point in that direction and give a sharp bark.

Then the young dog would go after the cows!

X1215.8. Lie: intelligent dog

4.

This is about the old fellow who lived in St. Peters. In those days—this was a long, long time ago—the bishop was in Arichat, you see. Well, the old fellow was a very pious man and he was very, very, very accustomed to observing every single holiday and every single holy day in the church, with every observance that was required.

So it came time for him to do his Easter duties. He always would go to Arichat and he'd see the bishop because the bishop gave better penance than anybody else. It made the old fellow feel super. He'd go home and he'd be in good shape, after Lent, and everything would be fine.

This went on for some years and then it came the year when the seat of the bishop would move from Arichat to Antigonish. The old fellow was pretty concerned at this point because he was getting along in years. So he went to the local priest and he said, "Father, I'm very concerned. I understand the bishop has been moved to Antigonish. Now, that's a good day and a half journey from here by wagon and a half-a-day's journey by boat. I'm very concerned that I won't be able to make the journey."

"Well," the local priest at St. Peters said, "I don't really think, Angus, you have to be too concerned."

"Yes, Father, I'm concerned. I'm getting near the end of my life and I want to prevent myself from going to hell, if possible."

"Well," the priest said, "Angus, it really is too far for you to go to Antigonish. Why don't you come to see me and I will give you some pretty sharp penance to do for Easter. You'll be in good shape."

"Dhia, dhia," the old fellow said. "What an awful choice I have. Will I go to hell by way of St. Peters or to heaven by way of Antigonish?"

J1260. Repartee based on church or clergy

5.

I'm reminded of a man that used to live on Holly's Hill. He and his mother lived there alone.

This is shortly after the time that catalogues came to be found throughout Cape Breton.

He brought this catalogue home and he was showing it to his mother. She was looking at all the wonderful things that she could find in the catalogue. There was harness and there was clothes for men. They were turning the pages and they came to the clothes for women.

Well, the son was perhaps a little less intelligent than the mother and he was looking at these pictures. These women in their underclothes. He was thinking, "I think I'll send for one of those."

So he went down to the office and he wrote out the order and he sent it to T. Eaton's, in Moncton. Every night he'd go down over the hill to Glendyer to see if the woman was going to come on the train.

The first day went and no, there was no woman on the train.

Then the second day.

On the third day he went down he said to his mother, "I don't know, I think there's some mistake. Let's check and see if we put down the right number."

She looked in the catalogue and said, "What did you send for?"

"Well," he said, "I sent for this one, to see would she come from T. Eaton's and help you and me in our home."

She just shook her head and very sadly too.

That night he went down to the station and there was a parcel came off the train from Eaton's. He opened it up and there was a pair of women's underclothes.

He rushed home, up the hill, full of great exhilaration. He went in and he said, "Mama, guess what? She's coming and she's sent her clothes ahead of her!"

J2450. Literal fool

DAN ANGUS BEATON

BLACKSTONE

6.

Malcolm Walker was telling me this one, you know, about old Donald and Katy.

They were very, very poor. Oh, they were as poor as could be poor and the old woman never had too many dishes in the house. There was never a dipper in the house and she always wanted one in the worst way.

Well, they were both in the house and a fairy appeared to them and told them, "Now, you two people are having it hard. You're good-living people and you're having it hard. You can have any three wishes in this world that you want but—make use of them. Any three wishes."

The old lady jumped up and she said, "Oh my God, I wish I had a dipper!"

Like that, the dipper was in front of her.

Well, old Donald got so mad, for wasting a wish on such a foolish damn thing as a dipper.

"Kate, ya damn fool, what's the matter with you? I wish that dipper was up your rear end!"

Just like that, the dipper was up her rear end.

And they both had to put their last wish, together, to get it out of there.

750A The Wishes

J2071. Three foolish wishes

7.

Well now, this one happened in Scotland. Hughie the Little Head. The reason he was called Hughie the Little Head is the fact that he lost about half his head in battle. He was a captain in the army and he always rode a horse.

He was married and he was to fight this battle in Scotland and he was wanting to know what was in the future for him. So, he went to see a fortuneteller and she told him, "If your wife will get up in the morning, early in the morning you're to fight this famous battle, and get you your breakfast and see you off and kiss you goodbye and be awful friendly to you, you'll win the battle. If not, you'll lose the battle and you'll be killed."

Well, he told her the night before the battle was to be fought that he had to be up early. He wasn't to tell her to get up or anything.

Morning came and there she was. She wouldn't move out of bed, no way. He was growling and going around making all the noise he could, to see if she'd get up and get his breakfast for him. No way. At last, he took his shoe and threw his shoe at her but he couldn't make her move.

So, he had to leave and, sure enough, he got killed.

After he got killed in battle, he used to go around doing a lot of damage. He was doing a lot of harm. He was taking people on horseback with him and, once they were taken, they were never seen again. They disappeared forever. This was going on for a long period of time.

Eventually, there was a giant of a man born in Scotland by the name of Ranald Young Allan. How he got that name was, there were two Allans in the family. Young Allan and old Allan and, of course, there's a long history to that but I won't go into it.

Young Allan got married and he finally had a son named Ranald. He was a very powerful man when he grew up and once, when he was travelling along at night, this man on horseback caught up with him, like he did with many others, and offered him a ride. He didn't know, at the time, who he was.

"Sure"—he was tired and he jumped on horseback with him. He had about seven miles to go. They only rode a short distance when he swung into the woods. A short cut through the woods. By golly, after the horseman swung into the woods, a moon kind of came out of the clouds and he noticed who had him.

They were going by a big birch tree and Ranald Young Allan put his hands right around the birch and around Hughie the Little Head and spurred the horse ahead. As he did, Hughie started to come off the horse and he had to stop the horse.

In the struggle, the horse loosened one of the shoes on him, on his feet. Hughie begged Ranald not to take him off.

He said, "You're coming off. You did enough damage here in Scotland. You're through with your damage in Scotland."

Hughie told him, "If you leave me on, I'll harm no one anymore but my life and death shall be with my wife's people as long as I live."

And I'm not going to name them either. There's some of you around here know who they are. Most of you do.

To this day, when people who are related—or are of his wife's blood—die, he is seen at those wakes. I know people where he's been seen at Mount Young and in our neighbourhood. You can hear the loose shoe on the horse, when the horse is trotting around, until this day.

And that's the story, as true as you're sittin' there. Hughie the Little Head.

E220. Dead relative's malevolent return

E440. Walking ghost "laid"

E581.2. Ghost rides horse **M341. Death prophesied**

8.

When the railroad went through, they surveyed the road three times, where the railroad was going. Three different times.

The second time, they surveyed it right where, or just below where, my grandfather's house was, over on the main road.

He said, "What are you fellas doin' here?"

They told him, "We're surveying the line and cutting the right of way."

He says, "You're crazy. This railroad is gonna go down near the brook. Way down in the marsh, in the meadow, in Black Brook there. Below the Campbells and down in the brook. Down through the woods there."

They told him he was crazy. There was no survey through there at all.

He says, "There's where it's going because I walked on it for about a mile one morning, when I was looking for the cattle."

And the third survey went right where he said, right by the brook. There's where the railroad went.

E535.4. Phantom railway train

9.

This is a story about an Angus MacFarlane, from Sault, Michigan, that I knew and was working with me.

He was in the army and, every day that he'd get up, he had a chum with him, a MacLeod fellow. This MacLeod was the neatest man that a person ever met or ever knew.

He kept his rifle so shiny it was possibly the shiniest rifle in the whole army. He kept it so clean and nice. He was always polishing his rifle.

This was going on for three years until, one day, he got up and he took the rag and he was going to polish his rifle and he said, "No, you're not worth polishing this morning."

And he threw it to one side.

Angus MacFarlane turned around and said to him, "What's the matter with you now?"

"Nothing at all's the matter with me," he said. "The old rifle's saved my life many a morning and many a day but not today. It's not gonna do it today."

"Don't be so foolish," he said. "Don't be so foolish."

Well, by golly, they got into action and shells started going off. The two of them were always together for the last three years.

Now, cigarettes were hard to come by and, when one of the shells exploded, they jumped into a shell hole and he took a cigarette and lit it. He only took a couple of blasts out of it, a couple of puffs, and he threw the cigarette away. Angus got up right away and said, "What's the matter with you, wasting a cigarette like that?" And he went about fifteen or twenty feet to pick up the cigarette that MacLeod threw away.

[Angus MacFarlane told me,] "Just when I got to where the cigarette was, another shell hit right where he was and blew him to pieces. If I'd been sitting alongside of him, I'd have been in pieces. It was him throwing the cigarette that saved me and, sure enough, what he was sayin' about the rifle. It's as true as the gospel."

D1812.0.1. Foreknowledge of hour of death

Danny Tompkins

NORTHEAST MARGAREE

10.

My father used to have a bunch of milk cows. In the spring, early summer, they're going to have a calf. The cows are pretty cute, they'd get through the fence, into the woods and have the calf. They'd come back home but they wouldn't bring the calf.

The cow would come home and my father'd say, "I'll milk the cow and you fellas watch where she's gonna go tonight."

The damn dog came along and stuck his tail right down in the pail of milk! My father could have hit him right across the barn!

The dog took off and you know what happened? He came back home with the calf suckin' his tail!

X1215.8. Lie: intelligent dog

Annie the Tailor MacPhee

THE CORNER, INVERNESS

11.

There was a certain place up above where I was brought up, at West Lake there, that they used to say bochans were there.

I used to go up to Hays River sometimes, to look after a person that was sick there. This night, I had to drive all by myself. A horse and sleigh.

Well, this woman was supposed to have seen a car go across the road. That was before there was ever a car on the West Lake road. Only horse and buggy. And she was supposed to have seen a car go across the road and roll over the bank.

This night, it looked like there was a storm coming. About eleven o'clock. So I told them, "I think I better head for home."

Of course they tell you that a mare can see things better than a horse can, you know.

So, I went down to the barn and I put the harness on the mare and I started for home. I was coming along the road and she was powerful enough. All of a sudden, the ears went up and she just stood right still there.

I was only about twenty-two or twenty-three then. Wasn't scared of nothing.

She stood still there. She was snorting and she didn't want to move.

I said, "Come on, girl, we gotta get home. There's a storm coming."

So, she started to move a little but she was keeping out. I looked on the side and, by darn it, there was a big thing on the road ahead of me. I just took the whip out and I put it on her and galloped right by what it was.

After I went by, what was it but a neighbour of mine after coming from the store and he was late getting away from the store. He was going home with a brown bag and a stick through it on his back. That was my ghost that night.

I stopped and picked him up and drove him home.

E535. Ghostlike conveyance (wagon, etc.)

J1782. Things thought to be ghosts

12.

This fellow had a son and he was a piper in the army. He was shipped overseas and his father worried about him and worried about him. He couldn't rest at night and he couldn't do anything without thinking of his son because, when they landed over where the fighting was, his closest friend was killed right there. Just as they landed there. So, he was worrying.

There was somebody had a ouija board and he thought, "It won't hurt to go and see this certain person and find out about the ouija board. Find out what's happening with my son."

So he did. He went and the ouija board told him his son was okay. There was nothing happening to him and he was going to get a promotion while he was overseas. He was not to worry one bit about him. He was going to be all right and he was going to come home the way he left, without a mark on.

Well, he went home and he never had a worry anymore. When the war was over the son came back without a scratch.

D1325. Magic object reveals future history

13.

We had a man up home one time and he was scared to death to move out in the dark. He wouldn't even let you light the lamp. He wanted to get out before it got dark.

The poor soul just had one cow and she would be dry in the wintertime. He used to take a stroll to our place and different places like that, for to get a bottle of milk for him for to put in the tea. So this time, he went over in another direction from our place and he went into the house.

Now, during the day, they had been cutting firewood and he had overalls on. They were wet when he walked out and it was after getting so cold, they froze. Every step he'd take, they were rubbing against one another, making a noise.

He took off running. He lost the bottle of milk, he pretty near lost his whole life. He just got into his house and fell on the floor.

Poor man. I don't think he ever saw anything in his life. Just scared that he would see something.

J1782. Things thought to be ghosts

K1887.2. Deceptive nocturnal noise

Archie Neil Chisholm

MARGAREE FORKS

14.

It was told on a clergyman. This neighbour of his was continually drinking and the priest was after him all the time to "try to go a little bit sober." But nothing seemed to do him any good and he still kept drinking.

On this particular occasion, the priest met him, and he was very, very drunk. After having a long talk with him the man said, "Well, if I could only just get about five dollars, that I could straighten up with, I'll promise you, Father, that I won't drink anymore."

The priest had quite a sense of humour, along with a sense of mercy and justice, and he figured, Well, I'll just try him. He said, "You pray. You pray to the Virgin Mother and you just might get your five dollars!"

At the same time, he put his hand in his own pocket and all he had was three dollars. He slipped it into this fella's coat pocket without him knowing it at all.

So, about two or three hours later—and of course the fellow did possibly what I'd do myself—he headed for the nearest grog shop and added to his jag.

He met the priest again in the afternoon and this time he was really loaded. The priest said, "Sandy, this is an awful shame!"

Sandy was at the point where he didn't know to whom he was speaking or anything else. He said, "Look, who are you anyway, talkin' to me like that?"

This clergyman answered, "I could be your Saviour."

"You're just the man I want to meet," Sandy said. "Tell your Mother she still owes me two dollars!"

J1260. Repartee based on church or clergy

15.

A friend of mine was telling me this story about two neighbours that had fallen out. I'm going to call them John and Rory.

John was telling the story about a bad dream that he'd had and it concerned the other world. He said that he dreamt that he died and, when he got to the pearly gates in Heaven, St. Peter asked him, "Are you mounted?"

He said, "What do you mean?"

St. Peter said to him, "All those who enter the Kingdom of Heaven must come mounted."

He didn't say what animal you had to be mounted on, horse or donkey or whatever it could be.

And he said, "I was lost. I was lost. I didn't know what to do and I was very discouraged. I started walking away from the pearly gates and who did I meet but Rory, my bitter enemy."

Rory was always tricky. He always could think up some scheme. And Rory says, "I'll tell you what we'll do. We'll both fool St. Peter. You get on my back and, when we get to Heaven and he asks you, are you mounted, you can say yes. Then he'll open the gate and we'll both get in."

So, sure enough, John got on Rory's back and he came up, on all fours, to the gate. St. Peter asked, "Are you mounted?"

John said, "Yes."

St. Peter looked out and he says, "Well, tie your jackass out there and come in yourself!"

F11. Journey to heaven (upper-world, paradise)

K2371.1. Heaven entered by a trick

16.

This is one that I heard on our friend Danny Chiasson and a friend of his. When Danny was a young man he was very fond of the sea. He and his friend went out fishing this day. They loaded up pretty well and, when they were coming home, they were away off Cape Mabou. They were out of sight of land and they couldn't see anything. A storm came up.

At first they weren't a bit afraid but, when the boat seemed to come close to foundering every now and again, they began to take stock of their past. And probably some of it wasn't just according to the sheet they'd like to see up there in heaven at all.

Danny was more hardy than his friend. He was fairly cool but he was getting scared too. His friend decided there was only one thing to do, and he started to pray!

He was appealing to the Lord in every way that he could. He was promising the Lord everything. He said, "Dear Lord, if you'll take us out of this trough that we're into now, I'll never chase another girl."

And the storm continued.

The next thing he promised he said, "I'll never drink another drop of booze."

Then Danny spoke up right away quick and he said, "Look, don't promise Him anything for me! I can see Margaree Island!"

J1260. Repartee based on church or clergy

17.

It was Archie Chisholm who was one of the parish priests in Judique that delighted in teasing. He delighted in teasing Donald MacInnis and doing things to get some strange answer out of him.

So, Donald came this day and he was freezing cold and everything else. The priest happened to have a bottle of whiskey in the house and he knew that Donald liked a big drink. On purpose, he poured out, oh, just a very tiny, little drink. Donald was looking at it and the priest knew what was in his mind.

He says, "Go ahead, Donald, drink that. That's beautiful whiskey. That's at least seventy-five years old!"

Still, Donald didn't take a drink.

He says, "Why aren't you drinking it, Donald?"

Donald says, "I was just thinking of how small it is for its age."

J1316. Very small to be so old

18.

One of the old-time hotels in Inverness was noted for how you'd suffer with the cold in the winter. There was very little heat.

In those days, when you stayed in a hotel overnight, it was usually to go out on the train in the morning, at seven thirty. There was always notice given to an old gentleman, by the name of John R. MacDonald, who used to pick up the passengers at the hotel and also pick up their luggage.

One particular night, this traveller was in one of the rooms and it was extremely cold. He got up about seven o'clock in the morning. It was snowing and extremely frosty.

Of course, Mr. MacDonald had one of those great big handlebar moustaches. He had driven down from home with the horse and sleigh to pick up the passenger. Icicles had formed on his moustache by the time he came in. He was almost frozen.

The traveller was just finishing breakfast. He looked at Mr. MacDonald and he said to him, "Which room did you sleep in last night?"

J1560. Practical retorts: hosts and guests

X1622.3.3.2*. Man makes use of icicles

19.

This is a story that I heard my mother tell long, long ago. For a long, long time, up until she was eighty-five or more, her memory was quite clear.

She was telling a story of this particular clergyman. They sent for him to give the last rites to a fellow who lived about five miles from where the church was at Margaree. This is the story she told.

Apparently, he left home to perform the last rites but the man died during the night and, the next day, this clergyman came to the house. He started to apologize for not having been able to reach the house before the man died. He said, "I got to a certain bridge"—I know the place very well. The bridge is not any more than five miles from here.

He said, "I got to a certain bridge and I could not get by. There was something that was stopping the horse every time. I tried walking by and there was something that was forcing me back. I could not do it!"

When he was through apologizing and telling the story, the woman asked him if he was crazy.

"You were here at two o'clock in the morning!"

Which was the exact time he was trying to get there.

"You were here," she said. "You gave the man the last rites of the church!"

Now, this was told as absolute truth.

E425.2.3. Revenant as priest or parson

Sandy Deveau

ST. JOSEPH DU MOINE

20.

There was a woman died and they were going through this woods, carrying her on their shoulders. Two or three men were carrying her on their shoulders. First thing they knew, they hit a tree and when they hit the tree they thought they heard some noise inside. So, they opened the casket—it was only a box, like you say—and, geez, she was still alive!

So they brought her back home and, you know, she lived for about two years. Then she died again.

They were goin' back to the same road and the old man was in back of them. When they got near that tree the old man in back hollered out, "Watch out for that tree this time!"

E27. Resuscitation by slinging against something

J1250. Clever verbal retorts—general

21.

The two fellows who went to college together—one of them became a mission father and the other guy got married and he bought an old, run-down farm. There was nothing on it at all.

He started working the farm, doing all he could, and he got the farm going pretty good.

All of a sudden, there was a mission, and who came to say the mission but this mission father he had gone to college with. The farmer noticed him there and he invited him to the house for supper.

After they got through supper they went out in the field and they were looking around the farm. He showed him the patch of potatoes he had and the mission father said, "You know, you and God has got a pretty good patch of potatoes here."

Then he was showing him the patch of turnips. "You and God has got a pretty good patch of turnips here."

And then he went along and, "You and God has got a good patch of oats here."

"You and God has got a pretty good patch of cabbage here."

And when he got through he says to the farmer, "You know, you and God's got a pretty good farm here."

The farmer says, "Yes, but you should have seen it when God had it alone!"

J1260. Repartee based on church or clergy

22.

These guys were in the woods, lumber woods. There was a Quebecer and a guy from New Brunswick. Now the guy from Quebec used to swear. Oh, he was an awful swearer. It was just too bad. He would swear all day.

One day he lost his watch, about eleven o'clock in the morning, and he started swearing. He named everything that was on the altar. All the way down. Oh, everything. But it's better in French, you know.

So this guy from New Brunswick was getting scared. He was a good religious guy, you know. He was getting kind of scared. He says, "My God! You shouldn't swear like that. My mother always told me if you'd lose something you had to promise the Blessed Virgin, like, a quarter or a half dollar."

So he says, "Alright. I'll promise her fifty cents."

After dinner, he kept looking for his watch. Finally, about five o'clock, he found his watch. It was still going. He picked up his watch, put it in his pocket and, "Now!" he says, "I promised the Blessed Virgin fifty cents!"

He takes the fifty cents out of his pocket and he throws it in the woods! As far as he could.

He says, "By son-of-a-gun! You made me look for my watch all afternoon. Look for your fifty cents!"

J1260. Repartee based on church or clergy

Colin MacDonald

WEST BAY ROAD

23.

They took in six or seven moose from the mainland in 1929 or '30. Malcolm MacKinnon was forest ranger and they put up kind of a barn for the moose and they put up a very high pen and they kept the moose there all winter. They were feeding them hay and oats and anything they could give them because they were wanting to get moose in Cape Breton at that time.

In the spring of the year they turned the moose out and they crossed the road here and there. There was three of them went up to MacIntosh's Mountain. One of them was shot but this bull moose was left and he was roaming around. There were a lot of apple trees at that time. Apple trees everywhere and he was hanging around the orchards. This John MacAskill and his sister was staying up there, nobody near them at all and the moose got quite tame. Whenever he'd see the old MacAskill or his sister going with a bucket the moose would follow them.

She went out one day for an armful of wood and the moose come up to her at the woodpile. I think she fired every bit of wood that was there at the moose, then she made for the house. They reported that the moose was cross.

Well, they wanted to catch the moose and take it away because it was the only one left. They didn't want to shoot it. So, they decided they'd put a rope on the moose.

The house is gone now but there was a window on the upstairs, on one end of it. They got the rope reins and they spilled apples on the ground below the window. They tied the rope reins to the bannister of the stair to anchor the moose.

By gosh, the moose came and someone put a loop on the rope and they got the loop on the moose's horns. The moose didn't mind that but, him swinging his head, he found it tight, and the further he went away the tighter it got. Finally, he took a jump and, as far as I understand, he took bannister and stairs clear through the window and out through the woods!

Whether that's right or not, that's the way I heard it.

Anyhow, they shot the moose, and that was the first piece of moose meat I ever ate.

H1154.5. Task: capturing elk

FR. JOHN ANGUS RANKIN

GLENDALE

24.

In the old days, they had these society bulls. They'd be stationed at different places.

So, this young fellow was sent with the cow and he was late getting back for catechism. It was finished when he got back and Father Donald asked, "Where were you?"

The boy told him.

"Couldn't your father do that?" asked the priest.

"Well, my mother thought the bull would be better," he said.

J2450. Literal fool

25.

Doctor Coady, in his heyday, was a terrific force you know. He came down to a meeting in Judique. He was trying to get the farmers all organized. Trying to get the fishermen organized.

He gave a talk and, at the end of his talk, he went into credit unions and co-op stores. He took a big slam at the big shots who weren't giving the farmers what they deserved to get for their products. At the same time, they were making interest on the money. And he went on like this for about half an hour.

An old fellow from Rear of Judique was listening and, when the meeting was over, he went home. On the way home, he was thinking about the talk and said to himself, "By God, I save all my slips. I better go over them and see what this man Coady's talkin' about."

So, he got home and he took down the slips for two or three years previous. He started going through the slips and, every so often, he run across this, "Ditto."

He'd turn another slip. "Sugar. Ditto, ditto"—and so on.

"Molasses and ditto." "Tobacco and ditto." He was there till three o'clock in the morning.

He went to bed and he woke his wife, Sarah. He says, "Sarah, what in the hell is this Ditto that you're buying?"

She said, "I'm not buyin' any Ditto."

"Well," he said, "I went through the slips and every one of them has Ditto on it."

"Oh," she said, "I thought that was something you were buyin' for the cows or the horses."

"No," he said. "I didn't buy any. I'm gonna see Coady tomorrow. I'm goin' up to see the merchant too."

So, he packed up his slips and headed for Judique glebe house but Coady had left for Antigonish. So, he went across to the merchant's.

"Come in the office," he says. "I gotta see you."

So the merchant went in.

He says, "Look, what's this Ditto? I checked with the wife last night. She didn't buy any Ditto and I didn't buy any Ditto. We never had Ditto in the house but every damn page here there's Ditto! We're payin' for that and we shouldn't have to pay for it!"

The merchant said, "Well look, this is what Ditto is. You come in, say last month, and you bought sugar. Instead of writing down sugar, below, I put Ditto. It means sugar. And the same thing for molasses on one page. Sometimes I run two or three days on the one slip and, if there was molasses again, I'd just mark Ditto, ditto."

Well, he was very humiliated over questioning the honesty of the merchant. He went out in the wagon, pulled the hat down on his head and started for home. A glum look on him.

He arrived home and the wife, Sarah, came out. "Did ya find out what Ditto was?"

"Yes! I'm Ditto. And you're a G.D. bigger Ditto!"

J1803. Learned words misunderstood by uneducated

26.

This fellow, Sandy, had a habit of going to church on Sunday, dressing up and then, on the way home, visiting the neighbours. Then coming home, still dressed in his Sunday best, he'd go to the pasture to pick up the cows and drive them into the cow yard. Then, down to the spring and bring up two creamers of milk that he had from the night before or the morning before and put them in the milkhouse.

He didn't have a lock on the door at all. He just used to, when he'd come to the door, reverse in. Then, when he got inside, turn around and put the creamers on the shelf.

Cousins of mine, Donald Angus and the rest of the gang, were devils for tricks.

Sandy had a cross ram. It was as black as the old devil himself. One Sunday afternoon these fellows thought of nothing better than going to the mountains and chasing the ram until they caught him. Then they brought him home and they put him in Sandy's milkhouse. He was cross to begin with and they started boxing him and he was heated up. Ready for anything!

One of them was keeping an eye on the window to see Sandy coming and the other fellow was still boxing the ram.

They saw Sandy coming with the cows. Put them in the cow yard, closed the gate, then he went down to the spring to bring up the creamers. When he was just about at the door, they knew he'd reverse in, they stepped aside.

The ram was back in the corner waiting for anything that came in. Sandy backed in with his rear end and the two creamers.

He got a paste from the ram and he was thrown about twenty feet from the creamhouse. He spilt both creamers and it got all over his clothes. He got up and saw this black form going by.

He headed for Donald Angus' grandfather's place and he said, "In the name of God, come over. The devil damn near got me. Bring the holy water!"

J1785.7. Black sheep thought to be the devil

27.

I was emceeing a concert, several years ago now. We had started the concert and, sometimes, I go in back to listen to some numbers I have lined up. This time, I was listening to Carl MacKenzie. All of a sudden I looked over at Bill Young. Bill was as white as a sheet, staring in space.

So, the number finished and he didn't say a word. I went over to him. "Are you sick, Bill?"

I kind of brought him out of the state he was in.

He said, "No. No. What's goin' on?"

"Well," I said, "Carl just finished and we're getting ready for another number. Shift the mikes around."

I got the second number ready and then, after a while, he came over to me. He said, "I've heard about you and ghosts. You believe in ghosts. Do you know who I saw out there?"

And the guy had died that winter. A MacLeod, from Sydney. Was in charge of a lot of work at the Highland Village. Bill saw him walk down the hill and come in just in front of the stage, then go in the crowd.

That's why he was in the trance when I happened to go over. He was just white.

E330. Friendly return from the dead

28.

In 1954 my father died. The day after the funeral I went around to the different people that he dealt with. There was a Malcolm Dan MacLellan, a merchant in Inverness, and town hall taxes. And I found out that there were only three bills that he owed and I paid these off and I went home satisfied.

I went back to the university and two or three times during that year—he died in April—there were times when I had eerie feelings about me that something was close to me that I couldn't explain. But I didn't see anything. I didn't hear anything.

Until the following June. A year later. I was teaching down at Xavier Junior and, after supper, I went over to Joe MacLean's, in Sydney, for some music.

Joe and myself played music from around seven o'clock until midnight. Then I went home to where we were staying. One of my brother priests was up watching television, so I stayed with him. He got tired of the show but I stayed till the end, then went to my bedroom.

I was the last room in the corridor and the switch was at this end of the hall. So, rather than go down and put on my own light, I shut the switch off and walked down the hall in darkness and went in my room. And I reached in for the switch.

When I did, my father was standing at the bed. I could see him from the knees up. I got a little startled and the first question I asked was, "Are you saved?"

He laughed at me. A smile come to his face and he said, "Yes, you know I'm saved."

I said, "What's bothering you?"

He said, "The bill."

By this time I'm getting my courage back and I said, "No. There's no bill."

He said, "Yes, there is."

I said, "Where is it and what is it?"

He said, "It's sixteen dollars and fifty cents I owe to Malcolm Dan MacLellan, the merchant."

"Well," I said, "I checked there and there's no bill."

He said, "It's there. Pay it."

I had a book in my hand that Joe gave me and I turned to put the book on the table. I turned back, there was nothing.

Well, I got scared then. So I sat up all night and I smoked cigarettes till daybreak. Then I went down and I said Mass.

It was bothering me all morning and after class I went to see the principal and I said, "Look, I'm going to Inverness and, if I don't find what I'm looking for in Inverness, I'm going to Halifax to see a psychiatrist."

I told him what it was and he said, "I've heard of that before but, in the name of God, don't tell anybody around here in the house or I won't have anybody staying with me."

He said, "You go and I'll take your classes tomorrow if you're not back."

So, I went to Inverness and up to Malcolm Dan's. Malcolm was busy. When the business eased up a bit I told him my mission.

He said, "No. Go away. I told you, when your father died, there's no bill here!"

I said, "Malcolm, if there isn't a bill, I'm going on to Halifax because I don't believe this stuff. I've gotta see the bill to have proof that what I heard or what I imagined last night is there."

When he heard that, he took me upstairs and we started going through old bills. We were there for a while and he had to go. So I went down and he said come back after dinner.

I went back after dinner and we started looking. Searching. We were there for another good half hour or maybe three quarters, and the son came along and said, "What are ya lookin' for?"

His father told him and he says, "Well, there's another box of bills. You gave me a bunch the other day, to be burned, and I didn't burn them."

I said, "Bring them up."

He brought the bills up and the third bill from the top was the one my father had mentioned. His name was there. Sixteen dollars and fifty cents. He told me how old the bill was and the date on the bill corresponded with the year he gave me. It was a ton of hay he bought in 1934.

At that time we had a cow in Inverness, as most people had. It was Depression and money was scarce and Malcolm always treated my father as a good, honest man who always paid his bills.

I paid Malcolm the bill and, from then on, I had no bother from anybody else.

E327. Dead father's friendly return

E351. Dead returns to repay money debt

MALCOLM FINLAY R. MACDONALD

MABOU

29.

I think we all seen lights long, long ago. I seen something similar to that right across from our house in West Mabou. 'Twas in the spring of the year, before the snow all left. There'd be sleighs, you know, but not too good for sleighing.

We were sitting to dinner and I said to my mother, "Look at all the sleighs is going up to the house over there." That was Rory Angus' house.

I was looking and she looked and she said, "I don't see no sleighs over there."

"They're right there," I said and I got up and went to the window. None.

When Rory Angus come over that night we told him about it. He used to come for a little ceilidh at night. Well, he laughed and he said, "If there was some old people over there you'd think there was somebody gonna die."

One of his little boys, Alec Joseph, was only two years old. That's the second Alec Joseph he lost. At bedtime he got sick with infantile paralysis and he was dead. He was dead before daylight in the morning.

I never went to the funeral but I saw my father and my brother going to the funeral. I think maybe my brother drove the sleigh that took the casket.

Well, that's the only thing I ever saw but I'd be praying after that. Good God, I didn't want to be seeing those things.

When Rory was over next time he said, "If you'd never told me that, that night, I'd never believe that you ever saw such a thing. But now, that's it. We can't help but believe you."

D1825.7.1. Person sees phantom funeral procession some time before the actual procession takes place

30.

A crazy thing I said to a fellow in Pictou who was from River John, outside of Pictou.

We got playing checkers, you know. He was a good checker player.

That night we got in conversation, playing the checkers. "By the way," he said, "where are you from?"

I said, "I'm from Cape Breton."

"Oh," he said, "I spent winters over in Cape Breton. Up by the big ridge back of Glencoe. And they're awful for ghost stories down there. They claim they see ghosts and all those things. Do you believe in ghosts?"

"Well," I said, "I don't know how to answer the question. I never saw a ghost and I can't say I don't believe in them. I can't say I do believe in them because I never saw any."

"Well, do you believe there's such things as forerunners?"

"Oh yes," I said. "There's forerunners on the bobsleds down home."

Well, that ended the story.

E723. Wraiths of persons separate from body

J1300. Officiousness or foolish questions rebuked

31.

This old Donald MacInnis used to come from West Bay, make the rounds through Judique, down to Port Hood and all around. He used to stop in Judique. He knew the old priest there. They were good friends but the priest used to pick at him a little bit.

This particular day he was coming through, it was blowing hard from the west. Little showers now and again, and he was getting a hard time. So he got to the glebe house in Judique. He come to the front door as usual and, when he got in there, there was two young, visiting priests at the fireplace.

When he saw this, you know, he just put a frown on. He didn't like it 'cause he always had such welcome and everything. To see those visitors, he figured it was going to be a different day all together.

The parish priest says, "Hello there, Donald."

"Hello, Father," he said.

"Where did you come from today?"

Aw, he was mad! "From Hell," he said.

"Well, well, well," the old priest said. "What's going on there?"

"Aw, the same as here," he says. "You can't get near the fire for priests!"

J1260. Repartee based on church or clergy

32.

Hector Doink was out for a walk and he came very close to a bear. The next thing he knew the bear was making for him, chasing him, and he took off running. He made for the first big tree that was there and he crawled up the tree. The bear was below but the bear didn't start crawling up after him. Hector was scared the branches would let go and the bear would have him. The bear took his time at the trunk of the tree there, waiting but, at last, the bear left.

Hector said to himself, "I won't go down in a hurry. I'll wait 'til that fellow's well out of sight."

That's what he did. He waited and waited until he went out of sight. He made sure he was well out of sight, and he started coming down, kind of easy, you know. When he got down to the foot of the tree he looked and here was the bear coming, with two beavers, to cut down the tree!

X1216.1(ab). Wolves tree man, go for beaver to cut down tree

33.

When Hector Doink got his call for the army, he paid no attention to it. He kept on cutting pulp in the woods. He had a pulp saw and an axe.

Anyway, he saw two officers coming in the woods, early forenoon, and when they came there he stuck the axe in a stump. They said, "You're coming with us."

They read everything to him and away he went. Left the saw there and the axe and the lunch can. Never even got home to change clothes. They took him right away with them. He spent three years overseas.

After he came back, he was visiting the neighbours and telling his experiences overseas and all this and that. Asking how people were here, back at home.

Anyway, he thought he'd take a walk out to the woods where

he had been working that day they took him away. He went out and, sure enough, he found the spot and there was the axe, still sticking in the stump.

Picked up the axe, looked at it, looked around and here was the bucksaw, still there too. And, behind a tree, there was his lunch can. Well, he picked that up too, opened the lunch can and opened the thermos bottle. The tea was still hot in the thermos bottle!

X1749*(a). Disregard for passage of time

Sid Timmons

NEW WATERFORD AND MARGAREE CENTRE

34.

I went in the mine when I was ten and a half, and I trapped a door for two days. That's opening and closing the door for the horses going in and out. The doors are for ventilation.

On the third day, one of the drivers got hurt, got a bolt stuck in his foot. I was used to horses around home so, naturally, I volunteered that I'd drive and, foolish enough, they gave me the horse.

And I always remember the first horse. His name was Diamond. One eye. And, if you spit in his face, he'd follow you around all day 'til he got a chance to rub it off on you.

He wouldn't bite you or anything, but just follow around and rub it off. Oh, yes.

P415. Collier **X1241.1(f). Remarkable horse: miscellaneous**

35.

In the week's pay, the overman would make up the pay, well—if you unloaded a box of timber, you got forty-seven cents.

That all went in as "consideration." Timber and consideration. You know? Was no set rate. It would cover a multitude of sins.

So, if you and I were working together, the only difference in your pay would be a ton of coal. The ton was never split in two. This week, you got the extra ton, and I got it next week. If there was an odd ton. That was the only difference in our pays, was the odd ton.

But anyhow, you and I got our pay and you'd always compare them, you know. We'd have the same, clear of that.

This fellow drew his pay and he had ten dollars more and his buddy said to him, "How come, b'y, ya got ten dollars? You didn't work any extra time."

"No, but I sold a cow to the overman, for ninety dollars. He's paying me ten dollars a week for nine weeks. Consideration."

He said, "That's fine. He's gotta pay me, too, or I'm gonna squeal on him."

So, the coal company paid a hundred and eighty dollars for the cow. That was just one of the small things. Oh yes, boy.

K443. Money (or other things) acquired by blackmail

K1271.1.4.3. Observer of intrigue insists on sharing in it (or enjoys the girl after putting the man to flight)

P415. Collier

36.

I had a dog. He was what they call a badger hound and he'd tackle anything. Didn't matter how big it was, anything. And he'd stay with it. He didn't know what it was to back off.

Anyhow, I was on the back shift all alone, so I decided to take him to the pit with me. You know, good company. So, I took him and, the first night, he got a rat. He grabbed the rat by the head, like that! And when he grabbed the rat, the rat grabbed his tongue. I had to kill the rat in his mouth. But he never made that mistake after. He could kill them.

Anyhow, he'd be with me all night and, while he didn't have a check number, that was all right, he knew every move, you know.

So, the first day I was day shift, Monday morning, I says to her, "Don't let this dog out till at least half past seven."

Now, where I was going to work, he had never been down there, and there was a door. He'd have to wait for the door to be opened to get through.

My brother and another fellow were rum sick, at a telephone, and about nine o'clock, this thing passed, you know. The other fellow said to my brother, he said, "Boy, I was drinkin' but I never seen a rat that big in my life! Did you see that?"

And my brother said, "Yeah, but it wasn't a rat, I don't think. It couldn't be, that big."

The dog. He was only about that high but he was about that long.

Well, it scared the two of them. They thought they were in the jigs then.

And he came down and, at ten o'clock, that dog found me. He waited till someone opened the door and he shot through it. And he was never down there before. Yeah.

That's the day I got mad at him and put him on a full trip and sent him up, to see if he'd be killed. Francis MacEachern said, when the trip stopped on the surface, he'd just dig a little hole in the corner of the box. He jumped off and shook himself and went to the washhouse. He was there when I come up in the evening.

J1750. One animal mistaken for another

P415. Collier

X1215.8. Lie: intelligent dog

37.

The pit stopped hoisting coal by night. Just what empty boxes were there, you'd get them.

'Course, this guy and his buddy had preference over me and my brother. We were driving two places and, of course, they were in the main place. They got the preference, you know.

So the day shift shot-firer came up and he said, "Sid, no use in you goin' down tonight, there's only fourteen empties." We'd need thirteen or fourteen a pair, and that's all that was there. He said, "The other fellows get the preference."

I said, "They won't tonight, b'y."

My brother said, "Let's go home."

I said, "No, we're not goin' home."

And, as you go down the slope, there's about two hundred feet of concrete, you know. There'd be worms on it and they'd be as blue and thin—you know—no nourishment.

I picked two or three of these worms—and I knew she'd put sausage in my lunch.

So, I made sure to sit with him and we had another thousand feet to go, from [level] nine to ten. I said, "Look, Ranald, before I get outta the rig, I'm gonna have a bite to eat."

I had the worms all the time, you know. They were getting pretty lively then in my hand.

I took some of the sausage out and chewed it up, and started to cough. I said, "Look...."

There was a squirt of vomit came out of that fellow, b'y. He vomited all over the fellow in front of him.

When the rake stopped he said to his buddy, "Let's go home. I can't work." And they went home.

My brother and I got the boxes. Yeah.

Many's the time I made him sick.

K1040. Dupe otherwise persuaded to voluntary self-injury

P415. Collier

38.

It was against the law, you know [to ride on a trip of cars designated for carrying coal]. But we'd be on it.

We come out and the overman was layin' on the main. We asked him, we says, "Is the pit done?" Saturday night, about half past ten.

He said, "No, there's a trip going up on one-ten."

Just as much to say, You can have your pick, y'know.

So, we went down and we got on it. And no one saw us gettin' on.

Anyhow, when we come up to the double road in fourteen, there was a flat spot, and he was one box behind me. I looked and I could see the sparks. Little sparks, y'know, from the wheels, coming towards us. There was only twenty-six inches between boxes and I hollered, "The other trip is comin', Johnny!"

He said, "The hell with the other trip."

And just then boy, flame! The other one jumped the road just above us. Of course, the trip we were on plowed into it. Well, I never knew I could jump off anything so fast till that night.

There was what they call a manhole. Every hundred feet in the deep, they dug a little hole in, about the size of the freezer, for an escape. But there was a timber right in the middle of this one. I jumped.

I went right across the empty track and right into the hole. When he went to get in, there wasn't enough room for the two of us, you know, and her grinding by. He was hollering, "Fer jeezus sake, get over and give me some room!"

So, everything stopped and the engineer called up the switchman and he said, "Two trips met."

He turned around and there were some men there and he said, "Two trips met and there's two fellas went up on it. You know what that means."

Well, some of them didn't want to go up and look for us, you know.

I remember Big Dan Cowans—he was killed after, not far from that spot—coming up from work, and when Johnny saw him coming he said, "Let's lay under the boxes and let on we're hurt."

I said, "Johnny, that's it, boy, we'll have to stay off of the trip."

"Yeah," he said. "We're gonna be killed on it."

K1860. Deception by feigned death (sleep)

P415. Collier

39.

They had—well, they had two but they got this third mule and they couldn't get her down [into the mine]. So he come along to me one evening and he said, "How about taking that mule down?" And I said, "All right."

I went out eleven o'clock that night. Instead of taking her down, I took her up on the bank head, you know. It was steep.

There was seven old fellows, big fellows, so I got them to push her till I got below the concrete. Well, the minute I got below the concrete, she was all right, you know. I took her down.

I spent two weeks with her on the back shift, alone, breaking her in. I got her down pretty good.

But she never moved till I stepped in the box and I never had to speak to her. The minute I stepped in the box she was gone.

This day, they brought an efficiency expert and they were touring the mine. There was the superintendent and the head engineer, general super, our manager—he was very sarcastic—and the underground manager.

We had a fellow by the name of John Alex Brown. Aw, he was a character. He could jig a tune—you'd swear to God it was coming from a violin. And there was a violin player two thousand feet above.

So, John Alex had heard a tune and called up this violin player. He wanted to know if he had it right. He was jigging the tune for him over the telephone. All alone.

When all these officials came down and they opened the door, right below—they could hear this music. Fellow going at it on the phone.

Anyhow, they come in, and I was standing with the mule hooked on and, when I'd go in with four boxes, after she passed four box lengths she knew, herself: she'd just stop, you know, and start backing out on the other road. I'd jump off and let her pass. Then I'd shift the track. Never had to speak to her at all.

They came along and the manager said, "There's one of your American pit horses."

The underground manager said, "Yes, and a hell of a lot of

good. She's good for nothin'."

Just as they went to pass, I stepped on the box and I crowed like a rooster! I knew the mare, she'd go anyway. And she left.

So, I stopped on the way in and I let them pass. When I figured they were just about into the inside end of the road, I went in and I jumped off, and the minute the fourth box passed, I started grunting like a pig. She backed right out.

I hooked her off and went out.

We were passing the office that evening. The manager called me in and this other fellow. He says, "We went down there today and we had strangers with us. When we opened the deep door, you'd think there was an orchestra down there. And what was it but one goddamn fool jiggin' a tune with two sticks."

He says, "We went in on the landing an' I thought we'd run into a damn menagerie! There was more animals runnin' loose in there."

He said, "If I hadda had a maul, I'da hit you two fellas in the forehead!"

He was embarrassed, you know.

K1200. Deception into humiliating position P415. Collier

40.

He come in one day and this Brown was jiggin' a tune with two sticks.

Fellow by the name of Tomerey had his pants off and he had a pair of gumshoes on the wrong feet. We had an old trapdoor and he was stepdancing.

There was two fellows boxing and I was refereeing—and I was supposed to be boss, road boss.

See, we had no overman over us. We were doing our work. We'd run like hell to get our work done, then wait. While we were waitin', see.

Boy, that was a bad day that day. I ended up on the receiving end on account of being kind of in charge.

K1980. Other impostures P415. Collier

41.

A pair of men had a narrow place to cut and drill the coal. You shot it, had a bite to eat, then you loaded it. You'd load twenty or twenty-two boxes, which was a good day's work.

These two Newfoundlanders come up rum sick one morning, a Monday morning. They said they weren't going to do much. Then they cut and shot two places and loaded forty-four boxes. Forty-four ton! And them rum sick! Imagine if they'd been feeling well!

They went to Number 2 mine in Glace Bay, where the high coal was. I guess the manager seen they were too greedy. There was two drivers for four pair. He took one of the best drivers, and he had a good horse, and he said, "You go haulin' for them fellas, alone."

Well, they come back to Number 14. My brother was boss there when they came, asking for work. He said, "I thought you were workin' in Number 2?"

The Newfoundlanders said, "Yeah, but it's no good over there. Ya'd starve to death. We loaded twenty-eight two-tonners without droppin' the shovel, and the pit knocked off. We hadda go home. There's nothing in that for us."

After they'd loaded fifty-six tons between them!

P415. Collier

X1080. Lie: occupations of remarkable man

42.

Them times, everybody tried to make a dollar but there was deep down friendship with everybody. And there was a lot of friendly rivalry. Even a man that hated you, if anything happened, you were injured or anything, he'd be the first man there to help. If you weren't hurt bad he'd say, "It's a pity ya weren't killed."

H1558. Tests of friendship **P310. Friendship** **P415. Collier**

43.

The pair of men above, you always tried to beat them. You liked to beat them a box of coal, if possible. It wasn't the thought of money. It was just that you loaded a ton more than the other fellow. That's one reason why there's so many old Cape Bretoners today, all bent and crippled.

You know, the Cape Bretoner had to be tougher, he had to be able to drink more rum than anyone else. You know? He had to be able to fight better than anyone else and he had to be able to load coal and cut logs and lift better than anyone else. And a lot of them, to prove it, injured themselves.

H1540. Contests in endurance P415. Collier

HUGHIE SHORTY MACDONALD

INVERNESS AND NEW WATERFORD

44.

This woman lived in Boston. She went away as a young girl and didn't have much education or anything. Just did a little housework or something.

When the end of each month would come, even with her last dollar she'd offer up prayers for, supposed to be, the nearest one to being out of purgatory. So the saying went.

By God, she got out of a job this time. There was no way of getting a job. She had no trade or nothing and, apparently, there was lots of girls coming who were taking up all the jobs of housework. So, she was after giving the last dollar she had and she was walking along a street, in Boston. This man came up to her and said, "You're lookin' for a job, are you?"

She said, "Yes."

So, he gave her an address and she went to this house. She

rapped on the door and the woman came to the door and she said, "I understand you're looking for a girl for housework."

The woman said, "Yes. How did you know? I never advertised or anything."

"Well," she said, "I met a man on the street and he told me to come here and I'd get a job."

So she said, "Good. Come on in."

The woman started showing her what to do and everything, and asked, "What did the man look like?"

The girl started describing him. He was tall and all this.

She was working around for a little while and she went down in the front room to do some little dusting, and she saw this picture on the wall. She called the woman down and she says, "There's the man that sent me here."

"Oh," she said. "My dear, that can't be. That's my husband and he's dead for about fourteen years!"

The girl said, "Well, that's the man that sent me here for the job!"

And the saying was that he might have been the nearest one to being out [of purgatory] and her prayers, this time, took him out, and he appeared to her for doing this.

E321. Dead husband's friendly return
E341.3. Dead grateful for prayers

45.

They thought it was time for this guy to get married. He was a little bit on the shy side and he was getting up to be about twenty-five. There was a girl about twenty-five miles away, and someone came up with the idea it'd be a good match.

At that time, they used to take a fellow along to ask for the girl's hand. So, they got a fellow to do the asking for him.

In the meantime, the fellow they got went somewhere and he saw this girl. When he saw the girl, the wheels began to turn. He had a nephew himself he'd like to see married to a good-looking girl. But, he was after promising he'd take this other fellow.

So, he fixed the thing up that, being it was so far with the horse and wagon, they'd go the evening before. They'd drive to within a mile or two of the place and stop off at this girl's sister's place for the night. They left, and him and the young fella slept together.

The wheels were turning all the time and, in the morning, he got the young fellow to get up and then—what did he do but he wet the bed!

He went down and he apologized to the people. Said he was very sorry, that he didn't know this fellow had bad kidneys or whatever it was.

Well, there was no phone but, right away, there was someone on horseback and went over to the other place with the word. The old fellow sent word right back not to bother even taking the fellow to the house. He wasn't going to have his daughter going to the brook every day with all the bedclothes, to wash them!

The outcome of it was that, in about six weeks or two months, he brought the nephew up and he got the nephew married to the girl.

K1218.9. Obscene tricks are played on simpleton who wishes to marry

46.

There was a woman dying in this small house. There was only one door coming in. There was a little room here and then you went up the stairs and one little room upstairs. She was up in that.

Apparently there was a couple of people, close relatives of this woman, that didn't want any clergyman coming in to see their sister. They believed it was all bunk. So, two of the brothers sat in a room, the kitchen, and they were going to see that there was no one going in to see their sister except the doctor. There'd be no clergyman.

So, they sat there.

Now, this man that brought the clergyman there with a horse and wagon or horse and sleigh—I don't know what time of the year it was—he knew that those people were there, and he told the clergyman, "If you need any help, give me a holler and I'll come in and help you out. If they try to stop you or anything."

He said, "Oh, you just set there and I'll be back in a few minutes." And away he went.

There was no disturbance of any kind. He came back and the fellow in the wagon said, "How did you get along? You didn't go in, did you?"

"Oh yes, I went in. Everything's all straightened out."

"You saw the woman?"

He said, "Yes."

The driver couldn't understand it and the brothers, till the day they died, swore that no one ever went by them. They never saw him.

D1713. Magic power of hermit (saint, yogi)

E425.2.3. Revenant as priest or parson

47.

Horse and buggy days, you know. This guy, oh my God, the equipment he had! Good fast horse, rubber-tire wagon and a yellow whip. You know, the fly-net over the horse.

He went to see this girl and I guess probably his intentions were, sooner or later, to pop the question.

She invited him to dinner and, of course, when you go to dinner, a special thing like that, they had all the best chinaware and everything on the table. So, he was trying to be polite and everything.

Just before they started to eat he had to go to the outhouse. Now at that time, they had buttons on the pants, the front of the pants. Anyway, he went out and when he sat back at the table he happened to look down and there was a button open. He saw this white thing like, you know, and he thought it was his shirt sticking out. So, he shoved this back in and he leaned over and he buttoned the button.

They had a big dinner and everything. He got up, thanking them, and pulled away from the table. He took every dish in the place!

The last they saw of him, he was running and the tablecloth

dragging between his legs! He jumped in the wagon and away he went. He never did return.

J2650. Bungling fool

Jim St. Clair

MULL RIVER

48.

A man who lived at St. Ann's around the turn of the century, he was a MacLeod and he was quite closely related to Dr. Frank MacLeod.

They had a rather large store just near the head of South Gut. Quite near where the Gaelic College is now. The old fellow had worked in the store for about sixty years. At the time this story happened he was seventy-five years old.

As it happened, there was a very attractive young lady teaching school in South Gut at that time. Her name was Jessie MacInnis and she came from West Bay. She was boarding quite near the MacLeods and was about seventeen.

The old MacLeod fellow began to be very attracted to young Jessie and he began to take a small sack of chocolates, out of his own store, in the evening when he'd go next door to call on Jessie. They'd sit in the kitchen and talk about what she did during the day and about the lessons and about the weather and about this and that.

She thought he was just, sort of being pleasant. An old man coming next door and visiting a newcomer in the community. But the sacks of chocolates began to get a little larger and MacLeod began to sit a little closer. Gradually, Jessie came to understand that his intentions were, indeed, matrimony!

So she said to him one evening, "Mr. MacLeod, I appreciate all the kindness that you've shown me since I came here to South Gut but I think you should understand that I'm planning to go on with my education. I'm going to college next year with the money that I have made here this year."

"Well, well," he said. "Jessie, that's fine but I'd like to have you just look at a paper I'm going to bring to you tomorrow night."

"That's fair enough," she said. "I'll look at the paper."

So he came the next evening and he had an awfully big box of chocolates this time. Not just a sack. And he had a very official looking document.

Well, it turned out to be his will and he said, "Now Jessie, I would like to have you read my will."

So, she took the will from this seventy-five-year-old gentleman and one of the things that she read was, "I, so and so MacLeod, of South Gut, Victoria County, do hereby leave all my worldly possessions, both real and personal, to be equally divided between my wife, the former Jessie MacInnis, and my son."

She stopped right there and she said, "Well, Mr. MacLeod, I really don't think I would plan to marry you right now but I'm quite surprised to see that you have a son. I didn't know that you were married."

"I'm not and I don't yet," he says. "That's the boy you and I are going to have after we're married!"

J445.2. Foolish marriage of old man and young girl

T52. Bride purchased

T91.4. Age and youth in love

49.

I think one of the most scary stories I ever heard about Port Hood involved a large rock with a ring, out at the end of a place called Sally's Reef. It's at the lower end of Port Hood, very near to Harbour View, and the beach makes a curve out there.

Some years ago there was a family in Port Hood by the name of Gruchey. The name, I think, has disappeared from the area all together. Mr. Gruchey had two very beautiful daughters, and he had one daughter who really wasn't very attractive.

Well, the eldest of the three daughters married and went off to live somewhere else and that left two girls at home. They got along awfully well, it seemed.

They were both, it appeared, to be of even temper and helpful to their father, who was a widower. Everything seemed to be going along well. They often walked out on the beach and each of them had quite long hair. They would sit out on the beach, combing each other's hair. That's the way I heard it anyway.

There was a man, a young man, came to work for Gruchey in the store. Gruchey was a merchant. Bought and sold fish. The young man had come there from River Denys. As it happened, he fell in love with the more beautiful of the two sisters left at home and they were engaged to be married.

One afternoon, perhaps some months before the marriage was to take place, the two sisters were sitting out on the rock and each one was brushing and combing the other one's hair. The less attractive of the two girls, at the end of the afternoon, was brushing and combing her sister's hair. While she was brushing and combing it, she was also braiding it.

And she braided it so that it was attached to the iron ring that was set in the rock.

It came late in the afternoon and the sister, who was attached to the rock, became quite fearful that the tide would come in. The other sister said, "Yes, the tide will come in and it will take you away and I will marry Father's assistant!"

As it happened, that was pretty close to what occurred except, as the less attractive sister was leaving the site where she was leaving her elder sister attached to the rock by the hair, she could hear her sister screaming at her. "You will regret it because you will see seaweed and the mark of the fish!"

The sister arrived home and she said to her father, "Something terrible has happened. My sister has fallen off the rock and into the water and I was unable to save her. Her hair became entangled in seaweed and I fear she's drowned."

A terrible storm came up that evening and they were not able to recover the body. In fact, it was some days before the body finally washed ashore on the beach.

Well, the young man who was engaged to the girl was heartbroken and, naturally, he turned to his betrothed's sister. She was very attentive to him and gradually, through time, he got over his grief and decided that perhaps he would marry the remaining sister. Perhaps too, he was fairly fond of his potential father-in-law's money and business.

So, the young man and the remaining sister were married. Some nine or ten months later, the young woman was to give birth to her first child. The midwife, whose grandaughter told me this story, who attended the girl as the child was born, screamed because she had never before been at the birth of a creature who came forth from his mother's womb wrapped in seaweed and with fins for arms!

And that was the mark. The curse put on by the drowned sister.

K2212. Treacherous sister

M411.3. Dying man's curse

M437. Curse: monstrous birth

S131. Murder by drowning

50.

This family near Glencoe Station—things were going along pretty well for them for a good many years.

There was a young woman in the neighbourhood and she was going to be married. So this particular family, that lived near the woman, they decided that they would put on a party for her.

About a week before this party was to take place, the woman of the house was in the kitchen and she heard somebody come in the front door and go up the stairs very quickly. She thought that was strange, there was nobody around. They were all away. She went down the front hall and she went upstairs. There was nobody there.

She just passed it off and, maybe a day after that, she was again in the kitchen and two or three others were around. All of a sudden they could hear the sewing machine, upstairs, going clickity clack, clickity clack. One of the old foot sewing machines, you know.

They thought that very strange and they went upstairs and the sewing machine had, indeed, been going clickity clack, clickity clack. They could see where the thread had come through.

Maybe a week or so just before the party that they were going to have, there was a kind of shriek came from upstairs. There was nobody there at all.

Well, came the day of the party and, in mid-day, they were all seated at the table in the kitchen having dinner. A wagon, that they did not recognize, drove into the yard and dumped off some boards, then went away.

They didn't understand why the wagon came in nor to whom it belonged or what the boards meant. But they were busy getting ready for the party so that was soon forgotten.

They swept out this outbuilding where they were going to have the dance and everything was in order. They had made the tea and gotten the food all ready and the thing was just going to be great.

The young girl had walked over from her own farm and she and the man to whom she was engaged were in the first set. As it happened, her father and mother were going to come on a little later. During that first set, the young girl collapsed. She was carried into the house and upstairs and she was put in a bedroom. She was very ill.

Not too long after that her father and mother arrived and they thought it was strange that the dance had stopped. So somebody went and told them that their daughter had fainted. The mother quickly ran up the stairs and, when she got to the top of the stairs and looked into the bedroom where her daughter was, she could tell her daughter was dead. And she shrieked!

There was no cloth prepared in the house to wrap the remains in, to take them home. One of the women that was there sat down at the sewing machine and sewed up the cloth. And that was the clickity clack, clickity clack, clickity clack.

The boards that the strange wagon had brought were used to lay out the body and take it home.

Ever after that, as long as the house stood, people were unable, really, to get adequate rest in it. The house has since been taken down and is no more.

D1827.1.2. Sounds heard before death; the sounds are later repeated in connection with the death or funeral

51.

I was thinking it would be a really good time in life to find one of those old-fashioned chests of money that are hidden here and there throughout the country. So far as I know, nobody ever really got hold of one. A lot of people have seen them. They slide underground and they seem to go somewhere else.

As I understand it you had to have an iron rod, tipped with either bronze or silver, in order to get hold of one of these chests full of gold coins. So far as I know there is still one somewhere up along the Southwest Mabou river. Not too far from Glencoe Station. I'm not going to tell just where it is because I'd meet you all there tonight.

You need to go, I think, at a time when it's quite a clear night and not much of any wind. It's a kind of formula.

At any rate, four or five people went out—oh, maybe about seventy-five or eighty years ago. One of them was a Moran and a MacDonnell and a Gillis. And I think there was a Cameron and a MacDonald. They followed all the proper procedures. They dug without speaking to one another. If you were to speak, then the chest would go "Choooooo," sliding along underground and you wouldn't find it that time.

They had the proper iron rod all coated at the end with silver coins which had been melted. They were getting along just great. They came down to where the chest was and they were just about to get it. Their hands were just about to reach down when some kind of night bird flew by. One of them just put his head up and said, "What's that?" And that was it! The chest went "Woosh," sliding along underground.

But left underneath the chest was a mat, a woven mat made out of some grasses, and they were able to pick it up. It was just the same size as an iron chest would be and they took it home to the house of Gillis. Gillis lived nearest to this place.

Now Gillis's house was one of those old-fashioned houses. You know, the centre chimney houses with three fireplaces in it. Mrs. Gillis was in the kitchen making tea, by the fireplace. The men were in the dining room where there was also a fireplace. They had spread the mat out on the hearth in front of the fireplace. Mrs. Gillis said to them, "Why don't you come into the kitchen and have your tea. There's a better fire in here."

They all went into the kitchen to have their tea and, just as they went through the door, around the corner of the chimney, there was a great "Swooping" sound. As though there were a lot of birds in the top of the chimney. The last fellow going through the door saw the mat, left lying on the hearth, go "Swoooosh," up the chimney!

No matter how many times they went back to that spot they were never able to find the right place.

And that little field, little meadow, is full of holes where people have been digging, looking for iron boxes full of gold coins.

D1155. Magic carpet

N542. Special conditions for finding treasure

N553.2. Unlucky encounter causes treasure-seekers to talk and thus lose treasure

52.

I'll tell you the story about the last sithean which were seen in Inverness County, so far as I know. The last fairies that were seen.

There was a fairy mound at the top of that Rankinville hill, Murray's Hill, in Hillsborough. And you can see that mound today, just below the road, almost in back of Galt Smith's farm.

Years ago, the fairies used to live there and they'd open up the mound every once in a while. They'd be having parties and they'd be having fiddle music and they'd be having songs and a few drinks. Sort of a good time. The people around there, some were United Empire Loyalist English and some were Scots, they sort of got along pretty well with them. They didn't bother them, and the sithean didn't bother them.

Now it happened that there was a man, who lived up in what is Rosedale today, by the name of Nosey John. He had a very long nose. He was a MacKinnon.

There was also a fellow in Mabou who was rather renowned for having a very long nose. His name was Malcolm.

Now Nosey John was starting out from Brook Village to go to Mabou one day. At the same time, Nosey Malcolm was starting from Mabou to go to Brook Village.

As it happened, Nosey John was coming along by the top of this Murray's Hill and he could hear the fairies singing away. "Sunday, Monday, Tuesday. Sunday, Monday, Tuesday." Oh, they were having a great time singing that song!

Well, Nosey John was coming along and he could hear this song and he said to the fairy people, "I can add some words to your song."

The lead singer amongst the fairies said, "That would be very nice if you could do that and, in payment for that, I will take off your long nose and give you a short nose."

So they sang, "Sunday, Monday, Tuesday" and Nosey John said, "The next two words are Wednesday, Thursday."

Oh well, that just made the little people so happy and they sang in English and Gaelic, and maybe French, "Sunday, Monday, Tuesday, Wednesday, Thursday. SUNDAY, MONDAY, TUESDAY, WEDNESDAY, THURSDAY!"

And, at that, Nosey John's long nose was taken off his face and he had a fine, short, handsome nose. Which made him very happy indeed. And he kept along down the road and, when he got to the foot of the hill, he met Nosey Malcolm.

Well, Nosey Malcolm was taken aback because here was Nosey John no longer very nosey. So Malcolm said to John, "How is it that you have a different nose from the last time I saw you?"

John told Malcolm, "Well, I was walking by the fairy mound and

I could hear the fairies singing Sunday, Monday, Tuesday, and I told them some more words to their song. Their song is now Sunday, Monday, Tuesday, Wednesday, Thursday."

Malcolm thought that what was good enough for Nosey John would be good enough for Nosey Malcolm. He continued up the hill and he could hear the fairies singing and the fiddle music was going and everybody was having a grand time. The little people were just in delight to have more words to their song.

But, the thing that Malcolm didn't know was that the little people don't like to have the end of a song. Because, if little people have the end of a song, it means they have to go away.

At any rate, Malcolm was coming along and he could hear them singing and he said, "I can give you more words to your song."

They said, "Well, that'll be fine."

He said, "You tell me the words that you know and I'll give you the rest."

So it was, "Sunday, Monday, Tuesday, Wednesday, Thursday." And Nosey Malcolm said, "Friday, Saturday."

At that point there was utter silence at the fairy mound. The lead singer said, "You have ruined our song. You have brought it to an end. In punishment, we will give you a doubly ugly nose."

And they took Nosey John's nose and put it on Nosey Malcolm's face. They closed down the fairy mound and, from that day to this, there has been no song from the fairy mound!

503 The Gifts of the Little People

F331.3. Mortal wins fairies' gratitude by joining in their song and completing it by adding the names of the days of the week

F344.1. Fairies remove hunchback's hump (or replace it)

J2415. Foolish imitation of lucky man

53.

Captain Hugh MacNevin was a ship's captain and he sailed some kind of a merchant boat out of Whycocomagh for Hong Kong. About seven or eight months after he left, there'd be a new MacNevin baby on the South Side of Whycocomagh and there came to be quite a family of them.

After about fifteen or twenty years of this sailing, he took sick one time while he was home and he asked his oldest son, John, to take the vessel and sail to Hong Kong.

He told the story afterwards that, when he arrived in Hong Kong, he went into a waterfront bar. He had a few drinks and he was kind of fiery and he got into a fight with an Oriental and he killed the Oriental.

He was taken immediately before a judge, who was an Oriental man. The Oriental man spoke English and he asked what offence had occurred and the constable stated that this captain had killed an Oriental sailor in a waterfront bar. The judge of the court said, "Your crime is very serious but, because you are a ship's captain, I will fine you two hundred and fifty pounds and will bar you from ever entering this port again."

Young Captain MacNevin took offence at this sum of money and swore, almost under his breath, in Gaelic, "You no good so-and-so chink!"

Which was immediately answered by the Oriental-appearing judge, also in Gaelic! He asked him, in Gaelic, "Who are you?"

John MacNevin replied that he was, indeed, John MacNevin from the island of Cape Breton.

The judge stood up, took him by the hand and said, "You and I are half brothers. Come home with me."

So, old Captain MacNevin had been busy both on the South Side of Whycocomagh and in Hong Kong.

N733. Accidental meeting of brothers

R155. Brothers rescue brothers

ARCHIE A. MACNEIL

CREIGNISH

54.

Hector Doink—Hector MacDonald—he froze one of his feet and he landed in the hospital in Inverness. Everybody that would go in to see him was asking him what happened to his foot. He was getting tired of this question.

There was a new nurse on duty and she asked him right away, "Hector, what happened to your foot?"

He said, "Well, were you ever to Midnight Mass, in Inverness, at Christmas?"

She said, "No."

"Well, I was there Christmas Eve and I was late. When I got there, the church was packed. They were even kneeling out in the lobby. I had to kneel down when I got in church and my foot was out the door."

X1623. Lies about freezing

ARCHIE NEIL CHISHOLM

MARGAREE FORKS

55.

This rich man bought a house. He and his wife and two daughters went to live in one of the very lovely residential areas of Nova Scotia.

One day, the two girls were out on the lawn and there were two boy friends with them. One of the girls said that she had some drawings and pictures and she was going upstairs to get them.

She wasn't coming back and she wasn't coming back, and her sister got angry. She went up and she found the girl in a dead faint on the floor! After a long time, she revived the girl and the girl pointed to a bedroom that was very seldom used. She said that when she came upstairs there was a piper, in full Highland dress, came out. He had the most savage look she had ever seen on a human being. She said he kept walking towards her and she couldn't move. She was just petrified. And the piper seemed to just walk right through her. She felt nothing and she went into a dead faint.

She went to see some old person and he said he had heard of that before and, sure as that piper would appear in that house, somebody would die very shortly.

Within two weeks, she was getting dressed to go out in the horse and carriage. One of the things the women often wore at that time was a hat and they used to use hatpins that went through them. She had a hatpin in her hand. She was running for something and she fell. The hatpin penetrated her head and killed her right there!

All right! About two or three weeks afterwards, the sister went upstairs. She had never seen this apparition before but, sure enough, the same thing happened. This horrible-looking piper came out of the same room and went through almost the same thing.

She went to run downstairs and fell! She got badly smashed but, before she died, she told her mother what had happened. The mother really believed this.

They had one son, away from home, and he came to live with the mother and he had a very beautiful baby. The mother just doted on this baby.

One day, the son and his wife went away on a trip and the baby was left in the crib. While the son's mother was standing there, she felt the most horrible sensation that a person could feel. She just felt as if there was nothing but an evil force around her. All of a sudden, she looked around and there was the piper! He was standing there and she felt so much under his influence. The only thing that could distract her was to look at the baby.

The piper slowly moved over to her and he took her hand.

There was a butcher knife there and he forced it into her hand. She was completely helpless.

Then, she seemed to be possessed of some evil force for a minute, just as if it was a reflection from him, and she drove the knife into her own grandchild that she loved so much!

All of a sudden the piper disappeared and she could stand there in nothing but complete horror.

Her son and his wife came home, only to find their little baby dead.

She tried to explain this awful force to them, this thing that happened, and she couldn't. They never believed her. They had her committed to a mental institution and, to her dying day, she repeated that story time and time again.

E265.3. Meeting ghost causes death **E425.2.5. Revenant as piper**
E574. Appearance of ghost serves as death omen

56.

Eddie MacLean and I borrowed a horse from Arthur Munroe. A horse and sleigh. We went visiting to a house up in Chimney Corner. It was in the wintertime. Lovely sleigh roads but there was a crust where the snow had frozen over the road.

Eddie was driving the horse and, all of a sudden, he nudged me with his elbow. He never opened his mouth, and I looked and there was this man, as true as I'm sittin' here, walking along by the sleigh. We couldn't hear him on the crust. He seemed to be floating rather than walking and he followed us, no matter how fast Eddie drove the horse. That man kept right along with us and right down to the turn of the road at Margaree Harbour.

Well, we didn't think too much of it until about a year afterwards. I was visiting a Mr. MacDonald's place, an old gentleman. He's dead now.

We were talking on different things and Mr. MacDonald was telling me about a peculiar experience he had coming down that road. It was almost identical to what happened to us with the exception that he said this man came right in over the wagon wheels and sat on the seat with him until he came right down to the end of the road where you fork down to Margaree Harbour. Then he disappeared out of the wagon.

And there was a lady came to see me afterwards. She asked me if this was true. I didn't want to scare her and I said, "Oh, our imagination." Or something like that.

And she told me the same thing had happened to her son.

E332.2(e). Ghost runs beside horses at night

E332.3.2. Ghost rides in carriage, disappears suddenly at certain spot

57.

A fellow—we're not going to say where he was from. He didn't have very much education. He went into a motel one night and he couldn't write his name. So the proprietor says, "Well, make your X there."

He made his X and then the proprietor gave him the price of the room for the night. And he says, "That's very, very steep. I can't pay that, that's awfully expensive."

But the proprietor says, "Listen, one thing you don't understand is that, with every room, there's a beautiful blonde that keeps you company for the evening."

This fella says, "Give me the pencil."

He took the pencil and he blotted out the X and he made an O.

The fella asked him, "What did you do that for?"

He said, "When I fool around with strange women, I never give my own name."

J2220. Other logical absurdities

58.

It goes back to the days when animals could talk. According to the early fortune tellers and philosophers of the old days, the animals could talk.

There was this group of cattle were out for the summer. When they were brought into the barn, in the fall, they were reminiscing over their summer. One cow is supposed to have said to the other, "What sort of a summer did you have?"

The cow answered, "We had a beautiful summer. We were eight of us in a huge, big pasture. The grass was up to our knees. We had a marvellous time and across the way, there was a fellow who kept bulls for sale and the bulls broke the fence down and that added to our joy of the summer. Personally, I never had such a good time."

But there was one little cow, down at the end of the stable and she wasn't saying a word. Finally, they said, "What was your experience?"

She said, "It was terrible. The worst experience I ever had. Forty of us were put in a six-acre field. It was scruffed off by the sheep before we got in there. We didn't see anything but ourselves all summer. Finally, one day, there was an ox jumped the fence. He spent the rest of the summer talking about his operation."

B211.1.5. Speaking cow

B299.2. Animals dispute

Paddy MacDonald

INVERSIDE

59.

You maybe know Hector and Neil Doink as well as I do, from working around the lumber camp.

Neil used to cook quite a bit and he got up on the mainland. He was around Truro for a long time and he wasn't coming home and he wasn't coming home. However, he saved up enough money to buy a car. He went and he sunk pretty well everything he had into buying the car and landed home with it.

He picked up his brother Hector and he says, "Hector, you're gonna get dressed up and we're gonna go tourin' the country."

So Hector did so, pretty proud to get in the new car. They went and they got a quart of rum and they started travelling. Up around Scotsville there, Neil noticed the gas was getting kind of low. He says, "Hector, have you got any money?"

"Not a cent," Hector said.

Well, they figured they better head back for Inverness while they still had enough gas. They were passing a farm and there was three pigs in the field. Neil stopped. He says, "Hector, there's our gas!"

It was getting close to dark and they got ahold of the pig and they set it in the back seat. They took off with the pig in the car, to sell in town and get enough money for gas. They come around a turn and who should they encounter but the RCMP. There weren't many cars on the road so the Mounties figured they better stop this one. So, they put the light on.

Neil went a little ways before he got stopped. One Mountie got out and came walking up to the car. He said, "Where you folks going?"

The bottle was still on the seat and they had no time to hide it. So the Mountie says, "You're havin' a few drinks. See that you go straight home. By the way, what's your name?"

Neil says, "Neil Doink."

"What's your name, over there?"

"Hector Doink."

"And you?" The Mountie glanced toward the back.

The pig went "OINK!"

The Mountie says, "Now see that you go straight home and no more drinking."

He was walking back to the car and he was lookin' back at Neil's car as it pulled away. He sat in the car with the other patrolman.

"Well," he says, "were they drinking?"

"Oh, they had a few in them but they're alright and I sent them home. You know, that Hector and Neil, I heard a lot about them. They're pretty fine-looking men when they're all dressed up. But their father there, Doink, is about the ugliest thing I ever saw!"

J1762. Animal thought to be a person

60.

I suppose everyone here got shafted a little bit, buying a horse or cow or something like that. You might pay so much for it and figure, afterwards, it wouldn't be worth it.

Anyway, Donald L. Dan was into the deal of getting calves and, for the last five or six years, he had four or five pretty darn good ones.

So, this year, he bought up some calves and he bought a cow with them. Right away I went down and says, "Well, Donald, what'd ya have to pay for it?"

"Three hundred dollars," he says.

"Three hundred dollars," I said. "For a three-year-old cow? That thing is worth about eight or nine!"

"Well," Donald said, "it's like this. They have milking machines and this animal was out in the mountain there feedin' on the brush. Feedin' on the hardwood boughs where Angus A. MacDougall was cutting. She was eating there all the time and she'd never come home. And the reason they didn't keep her there for a milk cow was they couldn't get the milk machine on it. So, I think if I tie her I can get enough milk to feed the calf."

I said, "Good enough."

Anyway, he left the calf under her and she was all right. She was never near a barn before, just out on the mountain all the time, browsing on small hardwood trees.

Donald had a contract in town for sodding and he stayed late one night. When he come home, there wasn't a darn bit of milk in the house for tea. So Anne says, "Donald, you're gonna have to go back to town and get some milk."

He says, "To hell with goin' back to town. We bought a cow and I got her tied in the barn. I'll go out and take enough from her to make some tea and for tomorrow."

So, good enough. He went out and he was milking and she was a great milker. She gave a whole, full bucket.

This was a little bit after dark.

Donald came in and what the hell did he have—but a bucket of sap!

X1203(a). Cow eats pine tops; the milk is so strong it can be used only for cough syrup

61.

This Liberal MLA died and went up to Heaven. He was pretty nervous when he come before St. Peter and St. Peter told him, "Sit down."

St. Peter opened the cabinet and pulled out a big file on him. Once he saw this file he started to shake right away. He must have done some hellish things you know, during his time on earth.

St. Peter would read a bit and then, every once in a while go, "Mmmmm, mmmm. Mmmmmm, mmmmm."

After about fifteen minutes it got pretty heavy on his nerves so he said, "Well, St. Peter, tell me, am I going to Heaven or to Hell?"

St. Peter went and closed the file and he says, "Look, I've been here a long time and I never saw anything like this while I been here. You must have lived a wonderful life while you were on earth. You lived such a good life that, well, while I been here at the gate, I never had a vacation and, you know, you're gonna take my place."

"Oh my God, St. Peter! I couldn't handle a job like that!"

"Yes, you can. You did pretty fair when you were on earth, handling things and you can handle it here. You gotta give it a try."

Well, he agreed he'd give it a try. Then he just thought, "Lord save us! I can't take that job. What am I gonna do when the Tories start coming through?"

"Look, boy, you don't have a worry in the world. I been here two thousand years and there wasn't any of them made it this far yet!"

J1260. Repartee based on church or clergy

62.

There was two friends. They always went around together and they worked together. One guy, he would save all his money and he went to church and he always put his money to good use. But his friend was a man of a different nature. When he would get his pay, oh, he would just spend it on booze and as fast as he could get rid of it, he would. You know? And then he'd be broke till next payday.

His good friend was trying to straighten him out. All their lives he was forever trying to help this fellow out and put him on the straight and narrow track. But he just couldn't do anything with him. However, they kept going around together.

Then, the good fellow got sick and he went to hospital and the doctors checked him over and they told him he was gonna die. Well, by gosh, he was awfully disappointed. You know? He took very good care of himself all his life. He was kind of puzzled. His friend there, he had drank so much and smoked and sleeping outside and everything, and he was as fit as a fiddle.

He called his friend and then told him, "Well look, buddy, the doctors told me I'm gonna die and I have no time to live like you have lived. So I want to ask you to do a favour. When I die, I want you to go to the liquor store and buy two forty-ouncers of the best whiskey that you can buy. I want you to take that back to the grave, once they cover me over, and I want you to sprinkle that all around the grave."

Well by God, his buddy that drank figured, what an awful waste! He says, "Well, yes, I'll do that for you. But would you mind if I passed it through my kidneys first?"

J1320. Repartee concerning drunkenness

X800. Humour based on drunkenness

63.

Two or three times, in the last

ten years, there was a woman appeared to me after I went to bed. Sometimes, I'd just be laying awake and this woman'd come in. I didn't pay too much attention to it, ya know. I was dead sober and all that. Then I told my mother about this woman and I explained what she looked like.

She was an old woman with a young face. There wasn't a wrinkle. And she had grey hair.

The last time I saw her I tried to talk to her and she said, "I'm going to see your father. Your father's going to die and he's coming with me."

So, she went into Dadda's room. I could see her walking into Dadda's room as plain as you're sittin' there.

Well, of course, at that time I thought Johnny Angus R. would never die.

I never saw her since.

Dadda went to the hospital and he told me before he went, he said, "Son, I won't be back."

I asked him, I said, "Did you see that woman that comes into my room?"

He said, "Yeah." He said, "I'm done for."

E425.1. Revenant as woman

E574. Appearance of ghost serves as death omen

64.

I was going out with a girl. Well, just kind of friends, you know.

Jimmie Smith had a girl friend in Port Hood and he would go up and pick her up, then come down and the four of us would drive around town.

There wasn't anything doing one night so Jimmie said, "Why don't we go down through the graveyard?"

I said, "I don't go along with that because you shouldn't defy spirits."

She looked at me and she says, "You're a coward."

I says, "Good enough. I'll go down through with you."

So, we went down. Jimmie was supposed to go through with me and, once we got there, Jimmie wouldn't go and his girl friend wouldn't go. It was about ten after eleven and I wasn't very fussy. I was scared sick!

I said to myself, "I won't see anything because I'm not doing this on my own."

We got about thirty feet into the graveyard, walking towards the church, and she stopped dead. Just froze!

I said, "What's wrong with you?" I wanted to get through and get out the other side.

She said, "Who's that over there?"

I says, "What d'ya mean, Who's that over there?"

She said, "There's a man, a big man, standing up there near the church."

It was a bright night. In the moonlight, I could see the shadow of your arm.

"God almighty," I said. "My eyesight's pretty good, and I don't see anything but the tree up there."

She said, "The tree is there but there's a man. A big man." She even described him from head to toe.

I said, "Okay, we'll walk towards it." I thought she was trying to scare me.

He disappeared. She said, "He's gone now."

Well, I just wheeled her around and I says, "We better get back to the car," and she took a fit. Screaming, hollering and falling!

I put her on my shoulder and that's the way it was for two hours. As I walked out I said to myself, "Now, she just got scared and all that."

I was scared stiff myself.

Lord God almighty! I was hearin' this SWISH, SWISH. Every step I would make, eh, there was another step in the hay. The hay would bend down but I didn't see the person.

I asked her afterwards, "Where exactly did ya see the person?"

It bothered me enough I took her down in the daylight and do you know where she pointed? Angus R.'s grave! My grandfather's grave.

E320. Dead relative's friendly return   E334.2. Ghost haunts burial spot

FR. JOHN ANGUS RANKIN

GLENDALE

65.

About three years ago, my mother died, and I was living in the glebe house, in Glendale, alone. There are eight bedrooms upstairs plus what's downstairs. So, the first night, I was a little bit shaky but I managed to get through the night. After that I was all right.

Two days later, one of my old neighbours came down and we were talking for a while and he said, "Are you stayin' in this big house alone?"

I said, "Yes."

"Oh, hell," he said. "It's not good for you to be alone. I'm coming down and stay with you tonight."

I said, "Oh, you don't need to."

"Oh yes, I'm comin' down."

He lived about three miles beyond the church and that evening, he walked down. He landed down about seven o'clock, come in and we were talking for a while. We played cards and told stories. Came time to go to bed. He was going to be upstairs, all alone, and I was going to be downstairs. So I said to him, "Listen, I'm not gonna leave you upstairs all alone. I'll go upstairs and sleep on the same floor."

"No," he said. "No, hell. You gotta be near the telephone. You stay where you are and I'm going upstairs."

So, we settled that. He went up.

I went into the office and I was only in about ten minutes or so and I heard an ungodly yell!

I come up and he was standing at his door, pointing to the floor and here his pants were coming along the floor just like nobody's business. They came around the bend of the stairs and they started down. I was standing at the foot of the stairs.

By this time, I got a bit leery myself so I said, "It's gotta be something natural or, if not, I'm gonna find out."

So, I went after the holy water and I went after the broom. If it was a spirit, I was going to use the holy water. If it was something else, I was going to use the broom.

When I came back the pants had come all the way downstairs and, when they got all the way to the bottom I heard, "Meow."

The cat had got on the chair where he put his pants and she got tangled up in them and she started down the stairs, with the pants around her. When she got to the bottom, she was clear.

You see, the point is, there are a lot of natural things that people are scared to investigate. They have natural explanations. Some of the ghost stories are that way.

J1495. Person runs from actual or supposed ghost

J1760. Animal or person mistaken for something else

J2614. Fools frightened by stirring of an animal

66.

There was an old priest in Judique, he was an awful man for tricks. This particular winter, the boy that worked at the place come in and said, "Look, somethin's happening to your hay. It's goin' down awfully fast and I'm not using that much."

So Father MacLean says, "I'll go out to the barn and we'll mark. We'll put down the hay that you're gonna need for the day and I'll mark the beams and posts around."

They did and they went out the next day and, sure enough, the hay was down about four inches below the mark.

So, they did it Saturday night. And Sunday, Father MacLean got up and he mentioned it during Mass. "I can't prove this but somebody is stealing hay from my barn. The fellow stealing it is gonna have the devil after him some night."

Monday, there was no hay disturbed. Tuesday, there was no hay disturbed. Wednesday, I guess the fellow was running low again so he came back.

Well, MacLean heard the guy coming. Remember these old-fashioned hay mattresses they used to have? It'd hold about a hundred and fifty pounds of hay. God, the guy came to the barn, went up the scaffold, put down the hay. When he got it down on the thrashing floor, he filled the bag and started off to the woods.

Father MacLean knew there was a pretty dark area he had to go through so he walked behind him and he had a pocket knife. He cut a hole in the mattress, pulled out some hay and, when the guy was in the darkest part of the woods, he lit the hay.

He was about halfway through the dark part, he looked back—the whole bag of hay was a blaze of fire. He threw the hay the hell to the woods and pulled off on the run.

He come down the next day and he said, "I'm the man who was stealin' your hay, Father. The devil damn near got me last night."

J1786. Man thought to be a devil or ghost

K1838. Disguise as devil **Q212. Theft punished**

67.

There's an old saying with the Scottish people, if a person wants to buy a horse or a cow you have, sell it. Because they have a tendency, even though they don't mean it, to desire that animal. If you don't sell, something's going to happen to that animal. The old people, they had cures for this, you know?

In one case I ran up against, this person had the prayers to say. You had to go and get water out of a brook or river over which both the dead and the living passed. In other words, a bridge on the highway.

You take that water and you drop a quarter in it and you spilt the water out. If the quarter stuck to the bottom of the bucket—really a wooden bucket you should have—then there was a curse on the animal. You got the bucket again, you did the same thing, and that time you said the prayers over the bucket. You spilt the water on the animal and you made the animal drink some. In two or three days' time, the animal was well again.

I've seen that done. I was called up to bless the horse myself.

M429. Miscellaneous ways of overcoming curses

M471. Curses on animals

68.

There's an expression in scripture that says you won't get to Heaven till the last farthing is paid. This concerns a character up the way of Broad Cove Banks.

He was a very kind man, honest man. Paid his bills to the best of his ability but, as you remember, in those days there wasn't too much money around. The man had a little fault: his memory wasn't very good. He'd borrow things and not return them, not intending to keep them.

Anyway, he was troubled a great deal with indigestion, and this night, one of my uncles was at the place plus two or three other young fellows. They were playing cards, and he had an attack of indigestion.

He used to take two spoons of soda in half a glass of water, stir it up and get relief that way. This particular day, the wife had been housecleaning and she had Gillett's Lye and she accidently put the lye alongside of the soda. He went in and it wasn't too bright in those houses—you only had the lamps—and his eyes was getting a little bad. So, he took the box of Gillett's Lye, instead of the soda, and he put the two spoons in. The fellows saw him mixing as he came out and he downed it. He was dead within an hour.

That was in the fall of the year and, after he died, the rumours were going around that they were seeing him around the farm, especially around close to the road. And I heard my grandfather and my uncle say they saw him one night.

They were going home from Inverness and he got in the sleigh—the old wood sleigh they had with the seat up in front and at the back. They seen him in the back part of the wood sleigh and he stayed with them for, oh, a good ten or fifteen minutes. But neither one of them would speak to him. Too scared.

Later on, this old man was coming home one night, on horseback, and he met him and he spoke to him. He discussed some of the things of the other world, but the only thing that was keeping him from God was the fact that he had borrowed brass knuckles. He told the old man, "You go in the barn and, at the ledge above the horse stable, over in the corner, you'll find the brass knuckles. They belong to So-and-so. You go and give them back and I'll be at peace with God."

The next morning the guy came down, went in the horse stable, put his hand up in the corner and found the brass knuckles. He took them back to the owner.

E332.3.2. Ghost rides in carriage, disappears suddenly at certain spot

E352. Dead returns to restore stolen goods

N332. Accidental poisoning

69.

My father knew this man very well. They worked in the mine together. Each miner was paid by the box. Each box had a number and it was tallied. So, if you and I were loading at the face, the driver came in and dropped off so many boxes. Say, 98, 99, maybe 34, 35, 36. You filled them. The driver took them away and you'd fill more.

My father's buddy had a habit of not waiting for the riding rake. If there was a coal rake going up and maybe she had ten or fifteen boxes and a couple of empties, he'd jump in an empty and come up. It was illegal to do it, so he'd jump off when the thing slowed up coming to the surface.

This night, they finished around nine o'clock. There'd be no more coal cut. The buddy says, "There are two empties here, I'm taking one." He jumped in the empty.

As he would get handy the top, he used to get out of the box and ride the bumpers of both boxes. He looked at, let's say Box 40, and he saw himself there, dead. He jumped off fast and came to the surface.

Next morning he went down and signed off. Quit Inverness

mine. He told my father why. "I saw myself in Box 40 last night and I'm not gonna be taken up, in Box 40, from Inverness Coal Mine."

He was idle for a while but then the Port Hood mine opened and they were looking for miners. He went up to Port Hood. He worked there for a year and there was a shortage of boxes. So, they sent down to Inverness for boxes and they took up a dozen or so. One of the boxes was 40.

A month or so later, he went down one day and there was a fall. He was killed and his body was put in Box 40, from Inverness Coal Mine, and he was brought to the surface of Port Hood Mine.

E723.2. Seeing one's wraith a sign that person is to die shortly

P415. Collier

Laura Aucoin

GRAND ÉTANG

70.

This young man, one of his women relatives died. A couple of nights after she was buried he went visiting. It was quite a ways from his place so, going home, he didn't want to go through the long road. He had a short cut that went through a pasture. It was going down a hill and was in the wintertime.

So, going down the hill, the snow was packed and you could just go on the path. On each side of the path it was so slippery that you couldn't walk there.

When he got to the top of the hill he looked down and, just at the foot of the hill, there was this woman, kneeling at the side of the path. Right away, he thought about the one who had been buried, you know. So he didn't like the idea of going down through the path and passing near that woman. He decided to turn around and go by the long road.

Just as he turned around, his foot slipped and he started sliding down the hill. It was no use for him to try and stop, it was so slippery. He was heading right for the ghost. What he thought was a ghost. He didn't want to see the woman so he just closed his eyes tightly, waiting what would happen.

First thing he knew, BANG! And he stopped. There was nothing else to do but open his eyes and see what damage he had done to the ghost.

He opened his eyes and what did he have in front of him? A half burned tree stump. It was black and there was a part of it that the moon was shining on so it made a white patch. A patch he thought was a white kerchief she had on.

So, that was the ghost he had seen.

J1782. Things thought to be ghosts

71.

In the old days, most of the people had enough to eat. Most of the men were fishermen or farmers so they had enough farm produce and fish to last for the year.

But there was always someone that will never work. They were going around, from house to house, begging for food. It was okay if they had plenty of food but there was some that didn't have too much, they didn't like to give it.

So this old lady—they were saying she was living up the mountain—she went to this house and they gave her something to eat. But they didn't have too much butter so they didn't give her any butter. She knew they had cows but, still....

When she went out, she went to the pasture and she passed her hand on all the cows' backs. And all summer, they were trying to make butter. They would churn for a whole day long and they couldn't make any butter. So, they thought it was a spell she had put on the cows.

There was always some old man that had the, kind of, remedies. I hear they would take a piece of red flannel, put needles through it, then boil it in milk. That was the cure for the witch or whatever it was.

That's what they did and, after that, they had all the butter they wanted.

D2084.2. Butter magically kept from coming

G273. Witch rendered powerless

72.

This man went to an old man's place and he left his horse there for about a week. The old man told him, "I'll feed your horse but I can't give him any oats."

So he kept him there and all the horse had was hay.

When the man went to get his horse, he told him, "I couldn't give him any oats. I have only oats for my own horse."

As he left the man said, "Well, from now on, all your horse will eat will be oats."

All winter he fed his horse with hay but the horse wouldn't even eat hay. All the horse would eat was oats and oats.

And, in the spring, the horse died.

G265.7.1*. Witch controls actions of horses

DAN ANGUS BEATON

BLACKSTONE

73.

Captain Ranald Tulloch MacDonald and Captain Angus Tulloch MacDonald, they both immigrated to this country and they were granted two thousand acres where the city of Halifax today stands. Then, they were called back to fight another war in England and, when they returned, the place was squatted on so much that they just couldn't do anything with it.

The government told them to take two thousand acres any other place in the province. They took two thousand acres in the Lake Ainslie area. And that's where the Tullochs of the Lake Ainslie area came from.

One of them was the father of my great-grandmother, and that's how the story came into our family of this Captain Black John MacPherson.

He had a certain battle to fight over in the Old Country and he travelled across Scotland for information as to how to fight this certain battle. He came to a crossroads and there was a school. The teacher told him one of the MacDonald girls was in the school and, Bein' it's in the afternoon, she can go home with you and show you where they live.

So, that's how my great-grandmother rode on horseback with him when she was about eight or nine years of age. She rode on horseback with this Captain Black John MacPherson.

When he got there, however, the MacDonald captain told him no way should he fight this battle. There was no way he could win it and that the honourable thing for him to do was surrender.

He said he'd never surrender.

So, in place of surrender, he sold himself to the devil. He called on the devil to come and contact him, which the devil gladly did.

Now, when the devil was leaving, the bargain was that the devil was to come twenty years from that very night, to claim him. Him and his soul. And he'd win all battles, including this battle that he was to fight.

The devil left him a big black dog. He told him, "Anyone that's in the army with you and that's not loyal to you, the dog'll point him out to you. All you have to do is ask him and the dog'll go up and put his nose on anyone that's not loyal to you."

The dog was only the devil too, as far as that's concerned.

The captain was winning battle after battle and the years were slowly going by. Several years before the time was to come—before the devil was to come—he built a castle. A huge castle, all of solid rock. The walls were seven feet thick with huge iron gates on it.

He built an upstairs there for himself and he got five hundred of his most loyal and most able soldiers to stay below and defend the doors so the devil couldn't enter. He put watchmen outside the castle to guard the gate and warn the ones inside when the devil would be coming.

Two of the men he put outside the gate was a Cameron and a MacDonald. When the devil came, they both ran.

I suppose anybody would run when he sees the devil coming, brave as they were.

They weren't to look back but they did, to see what was happening, and both were killed.

This Cameron was to be married to a certain girl and his ghost appeared to her. Now, she had knitted a scarf that he'd wear around his neck. He told her to take the scarf and measure north, directly north, from the corner of the house where she was living. Measure seventy lengths of that scarf.

There'd come an awful snowstorm that night. The worst snow storm in the history of Scotland. At seventy scarf lengths they dug in that snowstorm and they found his remains.

From his remains, forty lengths due east and they'd find the MacDonald's remains. Sure enough, they did. His ghost told her everything that would happen.

When the rap came to the castle gate the ones inside asked, "Who goes there?"

The devil answers that this was the ghost from Hell, coming for Black Captain.

They told him, "No way are you coming in here."

They were going to defend the castle.

He told them the best thing they could do was just flee and let him have the castle and let him have Black Captain.

The next morning, all there was left of the castle was a rubble of sand. It was all crushed into sand. The five hundred remains of the soldiers were all found in there.

The remains of Black Captain was never found. The devil took him and his remains.

They came looking for that story, from Scotland. They had knowledge of it and they came here looking for it.

It was Hugh R. Beaton and Hughie Gillis that had the story and the reason they had it: it'd be Hugh R. Beaton's grandmother was the woman that rode on horseback with that man.

And that's how the story came to be among our people.

A996. Origin of settlements
C331.3. Tabu: looking back during flight
E235.2. Ghost returns to demand proper burial
G303.3.3.1.1(a). Devil in form of black dog
G303.20. Ways in which the devil kills people
M211. Man sells soul to devil
M219.2. Devil fetches man contracted to him

74.

There was an old fellow in our area and he used to get 'round with a cane. A very handy man. He made a loom that they had in the house and a crib that they had in the house and various other things that they had in the house. He was very handy with tools.

He became very old and they were living on a pretty prosperous farm. No question.

However, the old fellow died. Shortly after he died, the people closed up the farm and left the home altogether.

We were wondering why such a wonderful home and farm should close up. You understand?

I was talking with one of the boys. We were having one or two drinks together. That's many years ago. I was in my early twenties.

The conversation was, Why in the name of God did the whole family leave the house altogether? Why wouldn't one of you stay on the farm?

This fellow was just having a few drinks and he told me, "No way. I'll tell ya, Dan, just why we left the farm. Every night, just at the hour of eleven o'clock, after the old fellow died, we could hear him coming, with his cane, on the platform. The door would open and he'd go into the bedroom where he died. He'd take a while in there and he'd go upstairs and he'd take a while whackin' away at the loom. He'd take a while rocking the old cradle and the other things that he was using. Then he'd go."

"Why in the devil wouldn't you put locks on the doors that he wouldn't get in?"

He said, "We put six or seven locks on and every lock we put on, when he'd come, it would fly open and he didn't have enough respect to close the door after him. Even in the wintertime. We'd have to get up after he'd leave and shut the door.

"So, we went to the priest and told him and the priest said, 'That man has to come back and serve such time to pay for his sins. Until that time is served, there's no one can ever stop that.'"

The house was left. It's deteriorated and gone to nothing. There's nothing there now but a cellar.

Where he's going now I don't know. There's no door to open and no loom to work.

E338.1. Non-malevolent ghost haunts house or castle

E411. Dead cannot rest because of sin

75.

I'm going to tell you a real, true story of the first Rankin that came over to this country.

He was my grandmother's grandfather. They landed down in the Coal Mines there, somewhere. He had sons, and one of the sons, when he grew up, he built for himself. He built the house first, before he dug the basement. You understand me?

After he built the house they were waiting to start building the basement.

There was a schooner anchored out and this little boat coming into the shore, for a whole week. And a little old man with a whisker on him, with three or four young men with him.

There was a big rock, and it's there till this day, down on the shore of the Coal Mines. He'd measure from that rock and, every time they'd measure, up the shore they'd come, right to the corner of the house that he had built. They'd come right to the corner of the house.

They were two or three days measuring and, every time they'd measure, they'd come to the corner of the house.

They paid no attention to them but, at the last of it, they didn't know what they were doing.

One morning they got up and half the basement was dug out. The house was on top of it. If they'd dug the basement a little while sooner, they'd have got the treasure. The house was built right on top of it. The mark of where the thing was taken out was right there. Right down in the Coal Mines.

N517. Treasure hidden in building

N563. Treasure seekers find hole from which treasure has recently been removed

76.

My grandfather, well, they came from the Coal Mines. They used to fish out of the Coal Mines. That's where my grandfather was born and raised and lived, before they moved to Black River in 1880.

However, there was a neighbour of theirs there and he got away from the church. He just turned to be a genuine atheist. He didn't want to hear the name of God in any way, sense or form. He didn't believe in God, or at least he claimed he didn't.

The three of them—my grandfather and my grandfather's brother and this fellow—they were out in a boat, fishing off the Coal Mines. It came up a terrible storm and, in them days, there were no gasoline engines. All you had was the oars and the sails. This storm was pushing them out and it looked as though they'd be gone for sure.

Of course, the two Christians got praying for all they're worth. The atheist wouldn't budge a bit. They were pulling for shore as hard as they could pull and gaining very little, if any.

Then, the sky darkened up and one awful thunderstorm came. It was an awful one. It looked like they were going to be gone.

They turned around and said to this atheist fellow, who was a very close friend of theirs and a neighbour of theirs, "In the name of God Himself, bless yourself and say a few words of prayer to see if we can get to shore alive."

"Ahh," he told them, "I'd sooner lose the arm from the shoulder than bless myself."

Well, that was all right. They finally got ashore.

He was married a month or two after and his first-born son had no arm from the shoulder!

And that's as true as you fellows are sittin' right there. The arm wasn't there.

M437. Curse: monstrous birth

Q220. Impiety punished

Q551.8. Deformity as punishment

77.

I'm gonna tell you a story about a young fellow, about twenty years of age, a neighbour of ours. He used to travel a lot at night. I had a half-ton truck at the time and, in order to take the family to church—we had twelve of a family—I had a bench made in the back of the truck. Whenever I'd catch up with him on the road, I'd pick him up. He'd jump on the back of the truck and I'd take him. When I'd be coming home, I'd stop at his gate and let him off.

However, several times I passed the gate, never thinking of him, talking to the fellows with me in the truck and he'd start hollering. I told him, "Look, from now on, if I be going by your gate, you just rap on the roof of the truck and I'll let you off."

Shortly after that, he got killed in a car accident. Died suddenly.

I was, one night in Mabou, playing cribbage, and I played until about eleven o'clock. On the way home, not thinking of anything, when I was coming close to this gate, the three raps came on the roof of the truck. I woke up and thought, "My God, I thought I heard three raps on the roof but I must have just been thinking, or something." And right then, the three raps came on the roof again. I stopped. I knew I had company. I couldn't see a thing. I stopped for about a minute or so and I left.

About a week later, I was coming home again, the same place. The raps came on the truck again and I stopped it. When I stopped, the door swung open. A shadow came in, right alongside of me. And this is as true as you fellows are sittin' there.

Well, I didn't want to reach across it and shut the door, I didn't know what to do. I certainly didn't want to take off into the woods because that'd be a worse place than where I was at.

The next thought was, hold your head because, if I get clear nervous and start driving too fast, I might kill myself. So, I just steadied right down, my nerve, and I started driving. I drove, oh, maybe half a mile, till I came to a crossroads. What was with me left.

Right after that, I made for Mabou. Maybe I shouldn't tell this part of the story but I will. I had some masses said for this one and, from that day till this and that's twenty years ago now, I've never been bothered since. And that's the end of that story. Definitely, I was carrying a ghost.

E332.3.3.1. The Vanishing Hitchhiker

E443.2.1. Ghost laid by saying masses

78.

This time, I'm going to tell you a story about a fellow who's very much alive today. He was the seventh or eighth of a large family. After his father and mother died, the family kind of split up and this fellow went to live with his uncle in Antigonish. Of course, he was the golden-haired boy of the family there. He was well liked and well he might be. He was a fine fellow in every way and every respect.

His uncle bought a car, an old Ford car of around 1920, so you know it's quite a while back. Perhaps you remember the old Ford cars that were run on the old magnetos rather than batteries. You might have headlights and you might not, due to the fact that the lights were off the engine and the bulbs were getting burned out almost as fast as you'd put them in.

But there was a box social in a schoolhouse about ten or twelve mile from where he was. So, several of the boys got together and asked him if he could get the car from his uncle and take them to the box social. They clubbed together and made up the huge sum, in those days, of three dollars to pay for the gas. The country was dry at that time but they told him, "We'll have all kinds of bull beer and some bush whiskey."

The night that they were to go, there were no headlights on the car. What did he do but he tied a lantern in front of the car and that was the light that they had.

On the way going, he was driving along and the boys was with him and they were singing songs. All of a sudden, when they were about a mile or two miles from where the box social was, his mother's face appeared in the windshield, right in front of him.

He told me this story many times.

His mother's face appeared in the windshield, in front of him. He immediately stopped the car and he asked the fellow that was in front with him, "Did you see anything in the windshield?"

He said, "I thought I saw kind of a shadow."

"Well," he said, "let's get out, after drinking all this bull beer, and answer the call of nature."

When he walked in front of the car here, about ten feet in front of the car, was an old fellow that used to drink a lot and he fell across the wheel track and was laying right on the road. Had he gone another ten feet, he'd have went over him with the car and killed him.

He told me a hundred times, "If my mother's face hadn't appeared in the window, I'd have been involved in all that trouble." So it goes to show that, even from beyond, a mother is still looking after us.

E323. Dead mother's friendly return

E332. Non-malevolent road-ghosts

E363.3. Ghost warns the living

79.

This is a story that happened in Black River and it happened in the '50s. At that time, I was shipping milk to Sydney and, in order to increase the quota of milk going to Sydney, I rented a vacant farm in the area. The vacant farm had a very good house on it; in fact, the house is very good until this day.

For a period of time, all spring and all summer, everything was going as normal as could be and, occasionally, I'd go in to see that there was nothing happening in the house, and there wasn't.

But it came September, early September. It was graining time and I had a lot of grain cut. It looked like it was going to rain the next day and I worked late, myself and the boys. So we were late going milking, to this farm, with the result that it was dark before we were through. While we were milking, I noticed that there was a light in the vacant house.

Well, the next day, I went in and nothing was disturbed and I couldn't see a sign of anyone being in the house. Nothing. I just figured somebody might have been in, for the night, and had a lantern or something.

Okay. Several weeks later I was digging potatoes and I was late again getting over to milk the cattle. As before, the light was in the house.

I said to the boys, "You fellas finish milking the cows and I'll go and see who's in the house."

I hadda walk five or six hundred feet to the house, from where I was milking. As I was going by the kitchen window, I noticed that there was a candle, in a candle holder, on the table in the kitchen. And, as I was coming to the porch door, I heard someone sobbing and crying in the house. This surprised me, that somebody might be sick, and I opened the porch door and I went into the kitchen and, sure enough, there was the candle on the kitchen table. So, I hollered, "Who's in here?" No answer.

I hollered again. No answer. Believe me, the third time, he'd hear me no matter what part of the house he was in! Still no answer.

I didn't know then, what to do. I thought I'd go over and take this candle and look around the house. It was only small anyway. When I got over to the table—this is as true as we're sittin' here—here was an old paper. An old *Antigonish Casket*. And in the light of the candle was the obituary of the very man that owned the place and the house that I had rented. I figured whoever was sobbing and crying was reading this thing. This had happened several years before, because the paper was old.

After I finished reading and I read the last of it, may he rest in peace, I said to myself, "I'm gonna take this candle and I'm gonna look around to see who's in here."

I reached for the candle and, like that, no light. I was in the dark.

At that time I was smoking, which I'm not today, and I had lots of matches in my pocket. I wondered what made the light go out so fast. I reached into my pocket and got some matches out and lit them. Go to light the candle, no candle. No paper. Nothing.

I found myself in the middle of the kitchen, in the dark. I found the time long to get out of there, to be truthful with you.

Okay, the next morning, I went there and I examined the house through and through. There was no paper on the table, there was no candle, there was nothing that could give a light, in that house.

However, as it was late in the fall and it was getting close to the time that I paid the yearly rent, for the use of the farm, I went to the woman that owned the place. Before I paid her, I told her the very story that I'm telling you people here tonight. She looked at me and she said, "Well, perhaps it'd be a good thing for me to give this money, that you're giving me, to the church and for the soul of the man who owned the place, that he may rest in peace."

I said, "That's up to you."

And I rented the place for several years after that. I never saw a light or heard a sound from that day to this. And that story's as true as we're here.

E338.1. Non-malevolent ghost haunts house or castle

E402.1.1.6. Ghost sobs

E443.2. Ghost laid by prayer

E530.1.0.1(c). Building seen to light up strangely at night when unoccupied

80.

If I'm not mistaken it was in 1938 my brother Joe came home. My mother was sick in bed, that's why he came home. He came home in the wintertime.

He was somewhat second-sighted. He saw several, well, different things that happened.

Catherine and I had three of a family at that time. He was out one night, in the neighbourhood somewhere, and we were all in bed when he came in. Going by the parlour—there was always a parlour bedroom in all the old homes—going to his bedroom in the parlour, there was a little white casket setting on the parlour table. Right in our own house, with a candle lit on it.

He figured it was one of our three children that was going to be gone, was going to die. He went and he told my mother, "Catherine and Dan is gonna lose one of their little children. Which one, I don't know." And he told her the story about seeing the coffin and the candle on it.

Well, this was all right. He left in the spring and my mother was up and around and, by golly, she was watching to see which one of the three in the family was going to take sick because she knew this was going to happen.

But shortly after he had left, a woman came living with us and she had two little children. One was only a couple of months old. Didn't he take sick? They took him to Inverness Hospital and he wasn't there but about a week or so when he died.

Her brother-in-law made him a little white casket and she wanted him buried in Mabou. So, I left Black River, went to Inverness, picked up the remains—not knowing anything about what he had seen—picked up the little white casket, and she told me to be sure and stop at the house on the way to the graveyard so the children home would see the little fellow dead.

I took the casket and I placed it right on the parlour table and she went and she placed a candle on it. Just as he had seen it.

Then we opened the casket, showed the little ones the little fellow who was dead, and closed the casket again. I had lunch and we left for the graveyard in Mabou.

Mother says then, "Now, thank God it wasn't any of the kids here. I can tell you the story."

She told me the story just as it happened and it's as true as we're here!

D1812.0.1. Foreknowledge of hour of death

E538.1. Spectral coffin

M341.1.2. Prophecy: early death

CATHERINE BEATON

BLACKSTONE

81.

Bill Nicholson, he used to stay many a night at our place.

One morning he got up and he said to me, "What were you doin' in my room last night?"

I said, "I wasn't in your room last night."

"Oh, yes, you were."

I said, "No, I wasn't."

And he started getting cross. "Yes, you were! You came into my room last night and you had a lamp."

There was no electric lights then.

"You put the lamp on the bureau and you pulled the bureau drawer open and you were rooting around there."

"Well, it couldn't have been me."

"It was your step. It was you!"

I said, "Well, okay."

I said to myself, "He's dreaming."

About a month went by. There was an old fellow, sick, in the neighbourhood. An old man, and he was living with his daughter. Just about dark one evening, I guess the old fellow died.

There was a servant boy, or something, at the house and she

sent him up with a note to me, asking for a lend of white sheets and candles and candlesticks.

It was dark, so I took the lamp and went down to that bedroom. I pulled the drawer out and got the sheets and stuff and, after I came back with what she wanted, I thought, "Well, Bill Nicholson must have heard me after all."

That's as true as gospel.

E723.6.1*(c). Wraith appears to person in bed in bedroom

82.

Donald J., the storyteller, one night he was at my father's home. After a while he says, "I had a funny experience the other night."

It was in the spring of the year and roads were bad, no paved roads. He had to go to Inverness for groceries and he had to walk. It was a long ways from Inverness to Dunvegan, and he had some groceries in a bag, on his back, and he was trudging along, getting tired and it was getting late at night. He finally came to the crossroads at Dunvegan and he looked up and he could see the mountain. He was so tired. He said, "I just hated to think of climbing that mountain after my long walk from Inverness."

Then he said, "With the grace of God, I wish I was on top."

He told my father, "All of a sudden, I found myself right on top of the mountain! I don't know how I got there but I was right there. I continued and walked the rest of the road home."

He said, "Now, what was that, what caused that? Was it good or bad?"

That's the question he was wondering about.

V59. Prayers answered—miscellaneous

MALCOLM FINLAY R. MACDONALD

MABOU

83.

This fellow was looking for a boarding house. He was a woodsman or something and he was getting a hard time with those boarding houses where they had bedbugs, you know.

Well, he went from door to door and this lady come to the door, and it happened to be the spring of the year. He asked if she kept boarders.

"Yes," she says, "I have room for one more boarder."

"Well, before we go any further, is there any bedbugs in this house?"

"Listen, man," she said, "myself and the hired girl did the housecleaning from the attic to the basement, and all we found this spring was one bedbug."

"Well, okay," he says. "I'll stay for a week."

She give him the price and everything, he paid her and come in.

In the morning, at breakfast, she says, "How did you sleep? Did you sleep good last night, Donald?"

"Oh, I did," he said. "But you know that bedbug you saw?"

She says, "Yes, what about it?"

"He died," the old fellow said.

"How are ya makin' out he died?"

"They were all here, at his wake, last night."

J1560. Practical retorts: hosts and guests

X1291. Lies about bedbugs

84.

There was a girl one time, she had

two boy friends. Nice looking girl, and the boy friends were nice looking. One fellow was Irish, the other fellow was Scottish.

She finally made up her mind that she'd have to do with one of them, but it was pretty hard to choose between the two. She met them one evening and she said, "Now, I'd like to meet you fellas tomorrow, right on the corner here, and that'll be the end. I'll have to choose one of you and I can't make a decision today."

Alright, she left.

Well, the next morning, the Irish fellow didn't go to work at all. He bought himself some nice clothes, shirts and everything, got a haircut.

The Scotch fellow went to work, early in the morning, and he worked hard all day. Never even took time to go to the bathroom all day. So anyway, they had to meet at a certain time, and he got home and he had a bite to eat and he rushed for the corner where he was gonna meet the girl.

The Irish fellow was there, spic an' span, all dressed up with nice perfume on him and everything else. Then the girl showed up—and the poor fellow that missed going to the bathroom was in trouble.

So the girl come along and she said, "Who's got that smell off him?"

The Irish fellow thought it was cologne. "I have," he said.

So she jumped and she grabbed the Scotchman and they walked away down about three blocks. She looked at him and she said, "I can still smell that Irishman!"

H312. Physical and mental requirements for suitors

85.

Johnny Neil had a sick cow and he sent for my father. Father used to go around the neighbourhood doin' all those things when there'd be sick cows or all those things that can happen on the farm. Johnny told my father, "Come and see my cow. I got a sick cow."

My father went up to his place and went to the barn, opened

the stable door and he looked at the cow. Looked her over for quite a while, shook his head and said, "This cow's not sick at all, I don't think. Look at the condition she's in. The cow is lousy, that's what's wrong with her."

"How in the hell could she be lousy when she was never in the house?"

W115. Slovenliness

X1296. Lies about lice

Archie Neil Chisholm

MARGAREE FORKS

86.

It was about a young clergyman that came into a parish. Whether he was priest or minister, I don't know, but he was assistant to an older one.

The day came for him to make his initial sermon and he was awfully nervous. So he asked his superior, "I wonder, would it be possible that I could take something, to straighten me out and give me a little bit of nerve?"

Well, the older clergyman said, "I don't know that I condone this but there is a bottle of gin in the cupboard. Take a little shot of that just before you're ready to go out and start the service."

So, he took a little drink and, when his superior turned his back, the little drink was having affect and he took a real snort.

He went out and he had a roaring good service!

When he came back, he asked his superior, "How did I do?"

He said, "Well, you did all right, but there are a few things I'd like to correct in your sermon. In the first place, there were ten commandments, not twelve. There were twelve apostles, not ten. And," he said, "the Trinity is the Father, the Son and the Holy Spirit. Not, Big Daddy, Junior and Spook!"

J1263. Repartee concerning clerical abuses

X445.1. Parson takes a drink of liquor during the sermon

87.

Hector Doink was a very active and athletic fellow and he used to talk about the stunts that he'd pull off when he was young. He was telling me one time that he was travelling in the state of Maine. He was cruising timber and he was admiring the trees.

There was one particular tree that he was looking at and he said he looked up and he estimated that, from the ground to where the first limbs were, it was at least forty-five feet. It was just a beautiful tree.

Just when he was attentively looking at the tree, he heard some crashing behind him and there, not five feet from him, was one of those big, brown bears, just beginning to rear up on his hind legs.

I asked him, "What did you do?"

"What could I do?" he said. "There was only that tree and the limbs, forty-five feet up. I took one spring in the air!"

And I said, "Did you make it, Hector?"

"Not going up. But I caught them on the way down!"

X1741.7*(e). Person jumps with disregard for gravity

88.

It's strange, you know, how characters like that would be outstanding, in every community. I know one particular fellow at Northeast Margaree, he was a violin player too. In fact, he was one of the only local violin players at the time and his name was Mose Murphy. He was extremely witty. He happened to be physically handicapped—his back was broken—but he used to teach school and he'd come home on Saturday. His father would always have the one job for Mose when he would get home and that was to crosscut the wood for the week, on Sunday. Mose hated crosscutting. He wasn't physically equal to it but he'd have to get with his father, who was a big powerful man and very heavy on the crosscut.

This particular day, Mose was getting very tired of it. He was working for about five or ten minutes and his father was just leaning on the crosscut and it was killing Mose to haul his end. Finally, he dropped the crosscut. His father says, "Where are you going Mose?"

He never answered him. He walked into the barn and he brought out an old saddle and he threw it on the crosscut in front of his father. He says, "Look Dad, if you're gonna ride on this crosscut, you might as well be comfortable!"

J1500. Clever practical retort

P233. Father and son

89.

I know that the gentleman involved wouldn't mind my telling the story.

This man decided that he was going to sow the oats in the old-fashioned way. Broadcast the oats by hand, that was the style. And he met this famous Hector Doink, who had been the parish wit for so many years. He asked Hector if he could sow oats by hand. Hector said, "Sure I can. I did it all my life."

So the man told him, "When you get to my place, you'll find the oats and there's a pail there, go ahead and sow the ploughed piece, back of the barn."

But he forgot to tell Hector there were two pieces that were ploughed. One of them had just received its spring quota of potatoes. He had planted the potatoes in that field and Hector, by mistake, took the oats and he sowed the oats in the potato field, right over the potatoes.

So, Mister Mac came home that night and he saw the field, he saw the oats spread over the field and he went into quite a rage. When he went in the house, Hector was casually eating his supper and he says, "Hector, what damn foolery did you have today? You know what you did? You sowed the oats right over the potatoes that I planted."

Hector said, "You don't know anything about farming. That's

the way they do it in the West, where I came from. They calls it mixed farming."

J2233. Logically absurd defenses

90.

There was a man and he owned a very cross ram. The ram had attacked him a couple of times so he decided that he was going to get rid of the ram, somehow. But he didn't want to do the shooting himself and he was very, very near-sighted. So, he got a friend of his, on this particular day, to shoot the ram. But, what he didn't know was that, the friend was almost as near-sighted as he was himself.

So, the fella came but, unfortunately, instead of taking a shot that would kill the ram, he had mistakenly picked up a shell that was loaded with birdshot.

In the meantime, about a quarter of a mile away, on a hill, there was an old lady, an old maid, living alone, and she was huge. Very, very big. And, in the spring of the year, she decided that she'd get clear of the winter longjohns. But before getting rid of them, she had to go into Inverness and she bought a pair of bloomers for herself. The old-fashioned ones.

She tried the bloomers on and they were too small for her. So what did she do but she went out to the barn and she filled them with straw. The bloomers were about three feet wide and she hung them on a branch of a tree. She was gonna leave them there, for a week, till they'd sort of stretched, and then she'd get more comfortably into them.

In the meantime, the guy that was gonna have the ram shot didn't want to stand around and see his animal being sent to the Great Beyond. So he told the fellow, "Now, don't you shoot that ram till I get up to Maggie's house."

He only had to go a few yards and he was out of the other fellow's vision altogether. He took very careful aim at the ram and he loaded the ram's north end, as he was goin' south, with birdshot. The ram went clean crazy and he started crashing his way through the woods. On his way through, didn't he hook the old lady's bloomers! Here was this thing, about half a human body, going into every branch of a tree that they'd come to and there'd be another rip come into the bloomers and there'd be more straw going out. They went by the owner just like a jet and, to his dying day, he always claimed that he had seen the devil pass him by, ripping Maggie to pieces and she was falling away in sparks!

J1785. Animals thought to be the devils or ghosts

X120. Humour of bad eyesight

91.

It's a story concerning a guide we had in Margaree and he's very well known, Duncan MacKenzie. Duncan was a natural wit but he was also a terrific guide on the river. And down right opposite the house here is the MacDaniel pool. It was one of the most famous pools on the Margaree and they caught a lot of salmon there this summer.

But during the early '30s, along with depression, we had a terrific drought. There was about three years that there was hardly a thing grew. The river was down so low that you could walk across almost, with a pair of gumshoes on, without getting your feet wet. But they'd still be fishing and Duncan would be guiding, but they weren't getting any fish.

He ran across one particular fellow, from the United States, and he was always telling about the fish that he had caught other places and the fish that he had just missed the day before.

He told Duncan, he says, "I caught a fish right in that pool the other day. I hooked one and he was at least twenty-six pounds."

Duncan says, "Well, that's nothing. I had a peculiar experience in that pool myself. I was coming down netting salmon one night, illegally of course, and I saw a lantern on the bottom of the river and the lantern was lit. I reached down with a gaff and I hooked the lantern and took it up—and it was a bright, new lantern, still lit."

And this guy said, "Come on now, Duncan, you never did such a thing. How could a lantern stay lit on the bottom of the river?"

Duncan looked at him and he says, "You take fifteen pounds off your salmon, and I'll blow out the lantern!"

1920H* Will Blow Out Lantern

X1301. Lie: the great fish

92.

Back in 1956 I ran an election. We're mixed politicians here so it doesn't make any difference. It was the custom in Inverness County to have a Protestant and a Catholic running. I was the Catholic and Al Davis was the Protestant, on the Conservative side. Rod MacLean and Clyde Nunn were the candidates on the Liberal side.

On this particular night they were up back of Judique and there was an old lady sitting down, back of the stove. And Clyde was a beautiful dresser. He had a habit of always dressing up with a black coat and a white scarf and all. When he'd come in quickly, you'd swear he was a minister or a priest. So, this old lady couldn't understand any English, but she was telling the others in the house that this was a priest and she wanted him to hear her confession.

Clyde couldn't understand one word of Gaelic but Rod MacLean could, and Rod turns around to Clyde and he told him what she wanted.

"What am I gonna do?" he says. "I'm not a priest, I'm not a minister—I can't do anything about it."

Rod said, "Hear her confession. If it was Archie Neil and he thought he'd get a vote, he'd hear it!"

J1370. Cynical retorts concerning honesty

J1766. One person mistaken for another

J2496.2. Misunderstandings because of lack of knowledge of a different language than one's own

NORMAN MACISAAC

CREIGNISH

93.

This old fellow from Arichat, him and his wife was going to St. Peters, to the show. The drawing card on the grounds was the biggest bull in Nova Scotia. They had to go in to see this bull.

So, the old fellow was at the gate with his wife and kids and it was ten cents to get in. The old lady reached in her pocket for ten-cent pieces and she got about eleven. But there were about fifteen kids.

So, by God, the old fellow at the gate, who was taking the money, said, "My God, those all your kids, mister?"

He said, "Yes."

"Well, you go right through," he said. "The bull would like to see you."

H1572. Test of fertility **X700. Humour concerning sex**

94.

Brother Alex, we had a trawl out. Two lines of trawl. We had lots of codfish salted home.

This fine day, we were out. We had lots of water and everything on the boat for lunch. We ran our trawl four or five times. We ran the two lines of trawl and there was a fish on every hook. Hake and haddock and codfish.

I said to Alex, "My God, we should go over to see the patrol boat. We might sell a few haddock. It's the best fish we got. They might buy a few."

It's the only fish in the sea the devil couldn't hold. There's three finger marks on his back.

We drove over to the patrol boat. I said, "Do ya want to buy any haddock or any codfish?"

"No," they said. "We get all our fish for nothing. Government is feeding us."

I said, "You wouldn't care to buy a few haddock?"

"No, but the mate here likes haddock."

I said, "Okay, we'll give him a few for a feed."

So, I threw four or five haddock up on the deck.

We had no cigarettes and we got seven or eight packs of Export A's. We were awful glad to get the cigarettes.

We kept on fishing and, at that time, they had them big crates. They'd hold two hundred and forty pounds. You know, they were inch boards.

Not like the crates today, only a hundred pounds.

But them old-fashioned crates, we had about seven of them, full of codfish and hake.

Jeez, there was a squall came up from the southern. We seen the breeze coming and we head her for Havre Boucher.

We drove into the wharf and they were buying the fish then. A half a cent a pound. So, we kept the haddock out and we forked eleven hundred and seventy-five pounds of hake and codfish up on the wharf. We kept the haddock to take home.

By God, here a couple of weeks ago, I was down at the mall there, back of Hawkesbury, in the Dominion store there. I was looking at a little piece of codfish, cut off the corner of a codfish. It was $7.50!

The little corner off of the front of the codfish. But it was fairly thick.

I was thinking of the eleven hundred and seventy-five pounds we forked on the wharf for six dollars and some cents.

The little corner off of the codfish was $7.50.

A2217.3.2. Marks on certain fish from devil's fingerprints

U84. Price of object depends on where it is on sale

95.

Stephen Graham died when he was around a hundred. One day, Stephen was sitting on a barrel of horseshoes in Hughie R.'s forge. There was a travelling salesman in the forge and he was listening to Stephen tell stories. Oh God, Stephen was telling some pretty good stories. At last, the salesman looked over and he said, "Mr. Graham, did you come over on the ark?"

Stephen said, "Hell, no. The Grahams had a boat of their own!"

F571. Extremely old person

X930. Lie: remarkable person's physical powers and habits

96.

I was going to a dance one time, the other fellow had the jeep. We were going along the road to a place called Devonshire schoolhouse, in Bermuda. There was a girl walking on the road with an awful pretty dress on her, full of roses. You could see her a long ways ahead of you.

We picked her up and, by God, we asked her where she was going and she said she was going down to a place called Flats Village, to another dance. Well, we coaxed her to go with us, to Devonshire.

The dance went on and this girl, she danced all night. She had a good time. After the dance was over, it was kind of cold. I gave her my army coat to put on. Driving from the dance, we come up around this turn in the road and there was an old house set back from the road. She said, "Here's where I get off." She got out right quick and I didn't get time to get my coat. She disappeared in towards the old house that was back from the road.

We were pretty near the army camp when I thought of my coat. When we got there, I went in and got a flashlight, came back out to the jeep and we went back to this corner where the old house was in off the road.

We went over to this old raggedy house and I rapped on the door. There was an old woman came to the door, after a while. I said, "There was a girl came in here by the name of Virginia Rose."

The old lady said, "No, there's no such a woman livin' here."

I said, "Yes, she come in here and she had my coat on."

The lady said, "There was a girl living here by that name and she died about five years ago. She's buried down the road here, about three miles."

We decided we'd leave and we drove into this graveyard. I was walking among the tombstones, jeez, I spied one with Virginia Rose on it. I looked and I seen my coat, folded up right nice, on her grave.

E238.1. Dance with the dead
E332.3.3.1. The Vanishing Hitchhiker
E334.2. Ghost haunts burial spot

D. A. MacInnis

CREIGNISH

97.

Well, I'm going to tell a little story about an old couple that lived out in back of the Margarees. Times were tough and he had a little sawmill. They lived on a farm and it was nothing but rock piles and briar bushes.

Anyway, this winter, there was an awful snowstorm. It snowed three or four days. When the storm cleared off, the old lady got up early in the morning and the sun was shining. It was beautiful.

Nothing but diamonds, all over the snow. You couldn't see a bush, you couldn't see a rock.

Well, she said, "Hughie, get up and see the beautiful farm you have today!"

J1540. Retorts between husband and wife
J1810. Physical phenomena misunderstood

98.

This tourist came through and stopped down here and he said, "Well, Mr. MacDonald," and he started praising the place—"but the roads are very narrow. Oh dear, very narrow."

"Yes, sir, they're narrow but they're terribly long," said MacDonald.

J1499.10*. Retorts about poor country

99.

There was a fellow up in Troy, they called him Alex R. MacDonald. He took a trip down to Long Point to see this old lady. She was pretty witty, a Mrs. Chisholm, and she didn't see him for a long time.

She was asking how he'd got along. He was married?

"Yes."

"You got a family?"

"Yes," he said. "First I had a boy, then we had a girl, then we had a boy, and then we had another girl."

"Well, well. You couldn't do any better with a pencil."

J1440. Repartee—miscellaneous

X700. Humour concerning sex

100.

Father Peter was looking for a two-inch auger. He had this fellow look all over the place but he couldn't find one. His uncle was living up on the hill. He went up there and said, "Uncle Alex, what's Father Peter going to do with that two-inch auger he's lookin' for?"

The uncle said, "I suppose he's going to make a hole!"

J1252. Quibbling answers

101.

A good friend of mine in Inverness,

Malcolm Burke, he was—like the rest of us—he'd be sick some mornings. He was pretty witty.

He was waiting for the liquor store to open one morning. He was there a little early, pacing the sidewalk, not feeling too good. An American car came up. The man wound down the window and called Malcolm over and started a conversation with him. He asked, "What time do your liquor outlets open here in Nove Scotia?"

Malcolm said, "Ten o'clock."

"Are you from around here?"

"Yes," answered Malcolm.

"What time is it now, Mr. Burke?"

"It's five to ten, and if that damn liquor store don't open in five minutes, I'll be known as the late Malcolm Burke."

J1320. Repartee concerning drunkenness

102.

This fellow was working down in Margaree and I guess fish was very plentiful at the time. It was fish in the morning, fish at noon and fish in the evening. He was there for a few days and, this morning, he packed a little suitcase and he was going out the door. The lady of the house said, "Where are you goin', Dan?"

He said, "I'm going up the river to spawn."

J1560. Practical retorts: hosts and guests

103.

They started the fishermen's co-op here, and Havre Boucher and Creignish were combined. They'd come over here and they'd go over there.

Anyway, there was a big meeting in Halifax. This fellow from Havre Boucher met these two or three bigshots. They asked, "Where are you from?"

"I'm from Havre Boucher."

"Where's Havre Boucher?"

"Right across from Creignish."

J1252. Quibbling answers

JIM ST. CLAIR

MULL RIVER

104.

There was an old fellow from the Coal Mines and he didn't go up to Mabou too much, but this particular day, oh, I suppose it's pretty near a hundred years ago, he came into Mabou. He went into Joseph Hunt's store and he said to Mr. Hunt, "Well, Mr. Hunt, what is new in Mabou?"

"Well, Sandy," he said, "I'll just tell you what's new in Mabou. We have a bank."

"A bank," said this fellow from the Coal Mines. "Well, well, well, that is something new for Mabou."

"Yes," said Mr. Hunt, "and it's right across the street, over there. If you want to get in you'd better go over right now because the banks close earlier than the stores. They close at quarter of six."

Those were the old banking hours.

So, Sandy went over to the bank and there was the banker behind the wicket and he was an awful proper-looking man. He had a waistcoat and a watch and a fancy Vandyke beard and, oh, he was very dressed up. He looked at Sandy, coming in from the Coal Mines, and he said, "Huh!"

Sandy said to the banker, "And, uhm, what is this?"

"It's a bank!"

"Oh," says Sandy. "And what do you sell in here?"

The banker looked back at Sandy and he said, "Well, we sell fools."

"Oh," said Sandy, looking all around and seeing only the banker behind the wicket, "you must have had very good sales because I see you have only one left today!"

J1350. Rude retorts

105.

This concerns Cape Breton and it concerns Cape Bretoners but it happened in Lynn, Massachusetts, on the 14th of December, 1963.

There was a cousin of ours was staying with us, in Lynn, at that time. A man from Hillsborough. And I think that he really was quite gifted, with this second sight or sixth sense.

At any rate one morning he came downstairs, this day in December, and he said, "I had a very strange dream last night. It was just, almost, a vision."

Well, you know, you say to people who have dreams, "Well, tell us your dream!"

And he said, "I dreamed—or I could see myself, it was more like—that I was home in Hillsborough and I was showing some visitors the view from the top of our hill. From John Smith's hill." And he said, "I was leaning out to point the view to them and, at that moment, I fell over the edge and I kept falling down and down and down. Just before I hit the bottom, I grabbed onto some kind of a bush and I held on tightly. I looked down and my hat was going down into blackness that I couldn't see. The visitors, to whom I was showing the view, were very concerned because they couldn't reach me, but one of the men took off his pants and he happened to be wearing suspenders. So, he could drop his pants way down, with his suspenders, and he kept jumping them up and down, with the elastic in the suspenders, until I could reach the leg of the pants. I just finally got hold of it and, with that, they pulled me back up to the surface. I just was getting over the edge of the hill...."

And we said, "What happened then?"

He said, "I really don't know."

Well, that was in the morning. That evening, kind of a dark and rainy evening, we had some visitors who weren't quite familiar with the neighbourhood. So my cousin, who was very familiar with the neighbourhood, he went with them, in their car, to show them how they could find their way back to the main road. They were Cape Bretoners but they were living in Watertown and they were going back there.

He showed them where the road was and they started off on their way. Apparently he went to go back to the house, which was a block or two's walk, and when he crossed the street a speeding car knocked him down. He was struck by the car and went over the hood of the car and was left on the sidewalk, bleeding. The car went on, it was a hit-and-run.

At the time, he was wearing a hat and we never found his hat.

He was then taken to the hospital and, because he was so bloodied by the experience, they had to cut away his pants. And his suspenders had made a mark on his body and they had to cut his suspenders away.

He hung between life and death for forty-eight hours. He'd sort of come to and say something, and then he'd disappear, kind of into a mist. And then he'd come back and he'd disappear again. Within two months, he disappeared. He died.

The whole dream seemed to anticipate, or the vision that he had for himself, seemed to anticipate what happened to him that night. The hat and the suspenders, the lingering, going back and forth.

The next day, I went in to see his aunt, who was in another hospital. She was an old, old lady of some ninety-seven years. She had not heard of the accident.

I went in to her and I said, "How are you, Aunt Molly, today?" I didn't know how I was going to tell her about this mishap. She was very fond of this nephew.

She said, "Don't ask me how I am but tell me how Theopholus is."

I said, "What do you mean?"

She said, "All night long, I saw that man walking between the house and the barn, as though he were home in Hillsborough, and

I kept calling to him, 'Come in, come in!' And he'd look at me and walk away."

She said, "He's been badly hurt."

D1812.3.3. Future revealed in dream

D1812.3.3.11 Death of another revealed in dream

106.

A great many of the early settlers of Mabou originally lived in Guysborough, Nova Scotia. Some of them were United Empire Loyalists and some of them were members of various British regiments who had been given land for service to the King of England. Amongst these very early settlers, in the 1780s, there was a family which had its origins in the island of Skye, although they had lived in the United States and had gone to the British side during the Revolutionary War. Another family that had been Loyalists had come to Guysborough, and a third family were amongst the few Lowland Scots families that came to Nova Scotia and eventually settled in Mabou.

The man from the Highlands of Scotland was a very powerful and very good-looking gentleman and he had spent a number of years in the regiment. As it happened, he was very good friends with the man who lived on the next property to his in the little village of Guysborough. A much younger man who had a very beautiful wife. Her name was Suzanna and her last name, before she was married, was Larabie. She was one of the most attractive women in early Guysborough and her husband was very much in love with her. So, it turned out, was the gentleman next door. This man from the Highlands of Scotland.

The young husband also had one small child, just a year old, and he had a very handsome pair of new boots which he had bought in the young city of Halifax.

In the grog shop in Guysborough, the retired veteran was heard to say one day, "It will not be too long before I will have those boots and they'll be under the widow's bed while I am in the widow's bed."

So, the young husband and the old veteran set forth one day, in a small pinkie. An early kind of coastal boat that they used to use here. Well, the next day, only one person came back. The old veteran. The young husband had, unfortunately, drowned. But, in some curious way, he had left his boots behind while he drowned.

The young widow took the boots home and she properly mourned her dead husband.

It wasn't more than six to eight months when the veteran had moved from his house to the widow's house and he was indeed wearing the boots and he was indeed placing them, every evening, under the widow's, now newly-married lady's, bed.

Strange noises began to be heard in the house, like kickings; and the boots, every day, would be moved from underneath the bed.

Mabou was just in the process of being opened up for settlement so, about 1792, the couple moved to the village of Mabou.

Now, many people in this room have driven down Mabou Ridge and have seen, in the distance, the elm tree up behind the present Mabou Church. That's where the couple settled when they first came from Guysborough. There's still a very large tree there and the foundations of a house and a barn but there's nobody living on the spot.

For the first six months things went pretty well but after that things really began to happen. Boots again began to move around the house, noises were heard upstairs and downstairs and the first child born, to the young woman and the veteran, had a very curious birthmark, in the middle of his chest, in the shape of a boot.

So, the couple decided that perhaps they should no longer live in this spot and they moved from there to a place further out, away from what came to be known as Mabou Village.

Things did not go well with them. A number of sudden deaths of young children in their family occurred. They were able, however, to give their crown lease to a land speculator who came from Halifax. He lived on the property for about six months and decided ha had heard enough knocks and bumps and groans in the night, and seen enough strange lights. He decided to sell the property, but before he was able to do so he drowned, very near to the present entrance of Mabou Harbour.

The property remained mostly vacant for some years with various people living there off and on. There never seemed to be much success for anybody who lived there.

The next family to acquire the property settled some distance away from the "noisy" spot where no crops would grow, but that family too has had its share of misfortunes. A number of very sudden deaths including a drowning.

There seems somehow to have been a continuing curse on that particular piece of property that may go all the way back to a young man, with a new pair of boots and a very beautiful wife, in Guysborough two hundred years ago.

E221.3. Dead husband returns to reprove wife's second husband (lover)

E281. Ghosts haunt house

E402.1.2. Footsteps of invisible ghost heard

E413. Murdered person cannot rest in grave

K800. Killing or maiming by deception

K1500. Deception connected with adultery

M474. Curse on land

S131. Murder by drowning

T563. Birthmarks

107.

Thomas Greaves, about 1840, was a poor stevedore in Glasgow, Scotland, and was working on the wharf of a very wealthy merchant. Greaves fell in love with the very beautiful sister of this merchant. He went to the merchant and he said, "I would very much like to marry your sister."

The merchant laughed at him and said, "You are too poor a man to marry my sister. You will never be able to marry her."

Greaves left and on his way out is supposed to have said that he would give his immortal soul if he would be allowed to marry the merchant's sister.

Well, it happened that Greaves prospered in the next few years and he was able, through hard work and perhaps some mysterious means, to amass a little money. He was beginning to engage in a wholesale trade and sending some things to Nova Scotia, but was still working pretty much for the merchant.

He went to the merchant a second time and the merchant said, "You will never marry my sister. She is of a class high above you."

Thomas Greaves is said to have struck the merchant who then landed on the fender of the fireplace and, perhaps, was killed.

Greaves took fright and ran out and down a long hill and, just as he got to the base of the hill, he could see a ship that was casting off its lines. He jumped from the wharf to the deck of the ship, which was on its way to Halifax. He looked back and he could see, coming out of the office door, the sister of the merchant. He could see, running down the hill, the policeman. Way up on the top of the hill, behind the merchant's office, there was a large black dog with fiery eyes, staring out at him.

Just as they were nearing the coast of Nova Scotia, an old sailor came to him at night and said, "Mister, I don't know what your troubles are but I know that there is something waiting for you in Halifax that you will not want to see. I would advise you, tomorrow night, under cover of darkness, to take the lifeboat that there is on this ship and row as hard as you can and see if you can find a place completely surrounded by water, an island, where no creature of any sort can get to you. When you get there, go as far inland as you can go."

Well, Greaves took the old sailor's advice and the next night he rowed and he landed at Ship Harbour which today is Port Hawkesbury. He headed inland and finally came to a place which today would be called the Upper Southwest of Mabou or part of Glencoe. He asked the people there if there was any land for sale. Somebody pointed in the direction of Mull River.

He followed that river along until he came to a plot of land surrounded by the lands of other people. Towards dusk, that first night, he made for himself a lean-to shelter out of boughs. Just as he was lying down to take his first rest on his own land on the Island of Cape Breton, he could see coming over the rise of the hill a large black dog with fiery eyes and the dog went, "Gruff! Gruff! Gruff!"

And for the next forty years, as long as Greaves lived, this dog went back and forth around the property line.

When Greaves took sick, about 1880 or 1885, he summoned the neighbours. He lived in a small frame house with a fireplace and he said to the neighbours, one of whom was my great-grandfather, "I want you to stay with me because I am going to die. When I am dead, I want you to bury what there is left of me, immediately, underneath the stones of this fireplace."

They sat with him all night and he died just towards dawn. They took the remains and put them out on the bed as though they were going to wash the body and wrap it in some kind of a shroud. As they were doing that, the body kept shrinking and shrinking until all that was left was the shape of a very small man, just about the size of a large doll. That's all that was left of Thomas Greaves.

Those three men were so frightened that they quickly wrapped what there was in the shroud, took him outside and dug a hole underneath the chimney. They buried him there and took other rocks and piled them on top of the grave.

They could see, standing on the edge of the clearing, this large black dog and the dog turned and walked away, barking as it went.

Now it is true that today, on a really clear night, I can stand at my back door and look across where Thomas Greaves lived and hear, "Gruff! Gruff! Gruff!" from a dog that does not exist.

E521.2. Ghost of dog

G303.3.3.1.1(a). Devil in form of black dog

H310. Suitor tests

M211. Man sells soul to devil

S110. Murders

Paddy MacDonald

INVERSIDE

108.

I used to go up, when I was young, up to Dan H. MacLellan's, and they had lots of stories. They were telling a whole bunch of stories that night and I was getting more scared all the time. So, I wanted to get out of there and head for home.

I got down to the main highway there and one of the stories they were talking about was the headless horseman. I just got out on the road and I looked and I saw this horse coming behind me. Well, I was after getting over the kind of tenseness, you know, after running all the way for about a mile and a half. So, I saw the horse coming and I figured, Donald's horse. Donald Ronald Angus, see, and I jumped on his back.

As he went along there was a kind of click in his shoe and I thought, "Funny Donald doesn't fix that, ya know. I'll ride him home and then I'll face him back towards Donald's."

We got to the end of the driveway. I got off his back and I tried to turn him and I couldn't. I thought, "He'll go home by himself." So, I started walking.

I was about thirty feet away from him when I heard, "Giddup!"

This horse is supposed to appear anytime that a MacLean dies, see. And there was a wake in town that night, for a MacLean.

D1812.5.1.22. Bad omen: seeing unusual sight on road home

E521.1. Ghost of horse

109.

We had a purebred ram. He was getting on about three years old. And we had one bad little devil there. Oh, he took after this ram we had there, fighting all the time.

I said, "Dadda, gee whiz, we have to kill that fella because he's only scrub and he's gonna kill the big ram."

He would hammer onto the big ram and the ram'd be laying on the ground there, just finished. We were wondering whether he was dead or alive. Dadda was scared stiff, you know, because he paid quite a bit of money for him. It would take maybe two hours to get the ram back up.

So I said, "I'm gonna kill this one the next time we're killing."

And we killed the young ram and cut the head off him. After we finished, down goes the old ram and he found the head. He was smashin' at it and smashin' at it.

I said, "Dadda, I'm gonna make a cup of tea."

Hector Doink came down the driveway and I told him the story about what the old ram had done. He couldn't beat the young one when it was alive so he was wearin' the head off the dead ram.

Hector says, "Awful what a ram'll do. I remember one time we had a cross ram home. If you hit him with a stick, then he would pound onto the stick. If you hit him with a bucket, he'd pound on the bucket."

This day, Hector was fencing and the ram was there in the field. He was looking at the barrel Hector was standing on, driving the posts. He come onto the barrel and knocked Hector down.

Well, Hector got mad. He took the hammer and he come onto the ram, right on top of the head.

Hector started home for dinner and he looked back and here the ram was getting up and he was hitting the hammer, hitting the hammer.

Hector thought, "I'll fix you," and he went and he put the hammer to a post and he went home for dinner.

Hector told me, "Upon my soul to God, [when I got back] there was nothin' left of that ram but the tail. And it was still hittin' the hammer!"

B299.1. Animal takes revenge on man

X1243. Lies about sheep

110.

Hector Doink stayed with us for a while. He had good stories. Then he went over to Waterford and, naturally, you miss his stories.

But one time he went on a little bit of a bender. 'Course, I would go looking for Hector in case anything would happen to him.

So, I picked him up this night and took him home. Next day he wasn't feeling all that well. He told me, "I had an awful dream last night."

I said, "What was it, Hector?"

"You know," he says, "I had a dream I died and I went to Hell."

I said, "Yes, and what happened then?"

"Well," he says, "I looked down there and it—it scared the devil out of me."

He says, "I knew that Angus and Allan, my brothers, died before me. I had that in the dream. And the first thing I did, my God Almighty, I asked to go to the bathroom.

"The devil says, 'Well, the bathroom is right down there, Hector.'

"So, I took off for the bathroom and it was an old-fashioned outside toilet, you know. When I got in there, I looked in and I saw something!"

"I went back to the devil an' I says, 'My God Almighty, I can't shit in there!'

"The devil sez, 'Why not, Hector?'

"'Well, when I looked down the hole, who was there but Angus and Allan, my brothers!'

"The devil sez, 'You go back, Hector, and shit in there because they shit on you all your life!'"

P251. Brothers V511.2. Visions of hell
X688*. Dream of finding townspeople in hell

111.

My mother's sister lived at home

there in Broad Cove. Maggie was her name. She was very good looking and all the folks around used to carry on with her. They would come in and they would just, you know the way you'd be, grab her by the shoulder or something like that.

One day she was sewing. She used to be a seamstress, eh? So, she had needles, used to put them in her mouth and, ah, this fellow come in. A neighbour. "Hi, Maggie."

She never saw him and he grabbed her right by the back of the neck. She went, "Aahh!" like that and down goes the needles!

And that's what she died from.

N330. Accidental killing or death

112.

Malcolm John MacPhail was, well, he was a very good friend of mine. He's dead now and his son is married to my sister.

They owned property down near the lake and they never fenced on the lake side, but they had fence around the top of the lake and around the sides.

So this year, they put a field of grain down there. After the grain come up they would find, my God, it was trampled. There was cattle getting in. They had young cattle down there but how would they be able to jump over that?

They started adding to the fence and still, same thing next day.

This went on for about three days, and then Malcolm John says, "Well, by God, I'm gonna stay up all night tonight and see which one of those heifers is jumpin' in."

One of them must have been awfully good because they were up to pretty near the seven-foot mark then and they had barbed wire across and there wasn't even a hair.

George MacKenzie said—George is a cousin of mine—he says, "I'll go with you because I can't figure out—the height of the fence, there should be some mark or a broken pole or something. We'll go down at ten o'clock."

Once they got there, wasn't there a big, white horse in the

field. So, right off the bat, Malcolm John was going to put the dog onto him.

And George says, "No. No. Hold the dog. Let's find out if he's jumpin' that fence or how he's getting in and out."

Malcolm John said, "That's a good idea."

So, they watched him for a long time and the horse was there until about daylight, munching on the grain. Once he got filled up, he went and he made about five or six big cow shits!

Then he jumped in the water and he swum back across to John Angus MacKinnon's farm on the other side of the lake.

F980. Extraordinary occurrences concerning animals

113.

This friend of mine came home from Toronto. We spent some time in college, Peter MacDonald. He was driving a transit bus.

This day, there was a group of guys come on the bus and he didn't know them. One of them didn't pay, so he told them that one of them forgot to pay and he had to pay.

But before Peter went out to Toronto, some years ago, he and I kind of kicked around together. We were very good friends of Long Charlie MacLeod, from St. Rose. Charlie died some years ago.

Anyway, those four guys on the bus started giving Peter a hard time and he knew he could get an awful pounding. They got up from their seats and they said, "Look, Cape Bretoner, this is the end for you. You're accusing us of not payin'."

They started up towards him, and Peter heard this voice towards the back end of the bus: "Leave that boy alone!"

He was telling me that the hair stood right on his neck, even before he connected the voice to who it was. [Long Charlie MacLeod came up the aisle and got off the bus.] Turned back, walked by the bus and he just made a little wave, like that. Like he always used to make.

Peter couldn't move the bus, he said, for practically an hour afterwards. He was so shocked.

Charlie was dead at that time, for two years.

E363.2. Ghost returns to protect the living

114.

This guy, a Newfoundlander, he won a lottery, eh—and he planned to take a trip around the world. Before he went, he bought pretty near everything he could think of for his parents.

After he started to travel, he got into some of those foreign countries and, by golly, didn't he think, "Gee whiz, that weekend comin' up is their anniversary." His parents' anniversary, and he was trying to figure out what kind of a gift he would send them.

He was travelling through all kinds of gift shops, and this day he was in a pet shop and what did he spot but a parrot. They told him that the parrot could speak. He started talking and, sure enough, the parrot could speak and it could speak eight different languages. Well, by golly, this is the present for Mom and Dad. He bought the parrot and shipped it all the way home to Newfoundland.

After some time went by, he landed back in Canada, so he decided he'd call his parents, see how things were going. His mother came to the phone. "Hi, Mom. How's everything goin' down home?"

She says, "Fine. Fine, George. Thank you for your gift."

He says, "By the way, how did you like it?"

She says, "It was delicious!"

He says, "You mean you cooked the parrot I sent?"

She says, "Yes, George. Why?"

"Well, that parrot could speak eight different languages."

She said, "Well, it's funny, he didn't say a word."

J1118.1. Clever parrot

J1820. Inappropriate action from misunderstanding

Hughie Shorty MacDonald

INVERNESS AND NEW WATERFORD

115.

We were down to a party in Margaree. This happened in about 1969 or something like that. We had quite a time and we left for home.

There was two cars and there was a young fella, from down the other side of the Island, with us. The fella's quite a piano player and he was awful interested in ghosts, you know. He was hearing about the Banks.

For years we used to stand in Inverness, as kids, and we'd look up the Banks and there was one big light and there'd be two little ones. One'd go to the shore and one'd go up to the road.

He was hearing so much about those things and he wanted to check on the ghost. There was only five of us going, so we got in my car and we left his.

Anyway, we got up so far and we were going around a little turn and there was a bridge there and he said, "Well, I don't see any ghosts."

All of a sudden the lights went out on the car. Four or five times. He thought I was doing this. So, I started turning around. I'm turning and turning and finally got turned around. When I started back he said again, "Well, I didn't see any ghosts."

My lights went out about five or six times and they stayed out the last time. I had to hit the brakes. So, I'm sweating pretty good. Then my lights come on and away I went. I come down from the Banks in a hurry! We dropped three of them off this end of Inverness and we started over on the pavement. He said again, "Well, I never saw any ghosts."

My lights went out ten times!

I said, "Listen, I'm gonna throw you out if you mention that word again," and I went home.

I'll tell you, it was a long while after that, I didn't go to sleep with the lights out. I got quite a start.

There was quite a few people after me, after that, to go back up. In fact, probably half the town was up the next night, you know. Some of them heard about it.

E272. Road-ghosts **E761.4. Life token: object darkens or rusts**

116.

There was one fellow, he was working in the level [of a coal mine]. You know, like the narrow works, making the road in and everything. He was down alone. He went down a little bit early and he was waiting for his buddy. He was drilling a hole with a jackhammer. There'd be a lot of racket and everything—and suddenly he got a hand drilling this hole. Well, he thought it was his buddy put his hand over his, helping push the drill in.

When he finished the hole, he turned around and there was nobody there. So, the guy quit the mine after that. His buddy died not too long after, but not in the mine.

But somehow, the buddy was giving him a warning of some kind. He just quit working in the mine and went away. Never went near a mine after that.

E336.1. Helpful mine ghosts

E336.1(be). Ghost warns miner of danger

E723.2. Seeing one's wraith a sign that person is to die shortly

P415. Collier

117.

You know, in the coal mine, you could be there all night, alone, fall asleep, and the rats running over you and everything. It didn't bother you.

I was driving a horse in the mine and all of a sudden, coming out where there were chutes where you'd load the coal, for no reason at all I started getting a funny feeling coming to this chute. Like, I kind of couldn't get warm, and a little bit afraid. And the horse I was driving, he'd kind of hesitate and, when we'd go by there, he'd take off like a shot.

So, every now and again, I'd have to load a trip there and the horse, he'd be just prancing back and forth. This went on for about a week or a week and a half.

When I went out to work this evening, they told me a fella got killed up in the chute that day. So I went down, the next night it was, and it was just like it was before. I had no funny feeling and it didn't bother the horse.

Apparently it was something that, you know, he could have been seeing something. And this feeling was going through me like there was something going to happen. I couldn't put my finger on it but, as soon as this happened, that was the end of it. It was just like before. I didn't mind going by, coming in or staying alone or anything.

D1812.0.1. Foreknowledge of hour of death

D1812.4. Future revealed by presentiment

P415. Collier

118.

A couple that lived in Deepdale—they were in Inverness and it was kind of stormy and kind of late at night. So they went down and they stayed in a house, one of the company houses. They slept on a couch down in the dining room and, God, they were just about falling asleep. All of a sudden the hall door opened. The man kind of looked to see if there was anyone coming. Nobody came. So he got up and closed the door.

Just about asleep again and they heard someone walking down the stairs, come to the door and open the door again.

This kept going, so they never slept all night. They were very happy in the morning when it got bright and they left. Probably five o'clock in the morning, heading for home.

They didn't want to say anything to the people of the house, you know.

Those people moved out and the people that moved in, they had a young fella there. I guess the poor little fella got nervous. This is what used to happen at night. He'd be upstairs for a little while and then he'd come downstairs and he'd open the hall door. There'd be nobody there so he'd just go back upstairs again. Close the door and go back up. He used to do this, probably, four or five times a night.

So, this is what it was. The forerunner of the poor little fella. He passed on.

E337. Ghost reenacts scene from own lifetime

E338.1(c). Ghost opens doors and windows repeatedly

FR. JOHN ANGUS RANKIN

GLENDALE

119.

In the olden days around here they used to have what you call hay frolics, wood frolics, milling frolics, spinning frolics and threshing frolics. This particular person, in Inverness County, had a hay-cutting frolic. He had lost the only horse he had, so the neighbours came and they were going to mow all the hay in one day. Which they did. They had a good time mowing.

The owner of the farm decided to have a frolic that night. "You fellas go home, get cleaned up and come back."

There were two violin players in the area so he brought them down. They danced then till two or three o'clock in the morning.

They broke it up but the farmer told the violin players, "You fellas stay till the crowd all leave and I'll drive you home in the truck."

He took the two violin players home, drove them to the door and started back home. The old fellows went right in and went to bed, after their prayers. They heard a rap at the door so one of the men raised the window and, down at the door, he saw the man who had brought them home. The violin player called down, "What's the matter? You have a flat tire or something?"

The man below answered, "No. I turned the truck over, on the way home, and I killed myself. I want you to go down and see the merchant. There's a bill there I owe. You pay that."

The fellow in bed could hear one voice, he wasn't hearing the other. "Who's there?"

The one at the window said, "There's something wrong. We'd better get up and get dressed and go back down."

They got up, lit the lanterns and got dressed. They were the first at the scene of the accident.

He had overdriven his own driveway, put on the brakes and lost control on the loose gravel. The truck turned over and he was killed instantly.

The violin player went down the next day to see this merchant. "Does this man owe you money?"

The merchant checked and said, "Yes," and showed him the figure. He paid it.

E351. Dead returns to repay money debt

E723.6.1*. Death-announcing wraith appears in or near building

120.

Big Eugene MacDonald, he had second sight. I was in Boisdale at the time and I used to go down to the station and sit a while with Gene. He was a terrific character. He knew a lot of people. He'd been station agent in different areas and he had lots of stories. If a situation was kind of grim or dull, go down and see Gene and he'd get you out of the mood.

This particular morning, a Friday, Gene had a long face on him. I said, "Gene, what's the matter?"

You had to know Gene and how to take him.

He turned around, "None of your business!"

I said, "Maybe it isn't, Gene, but I think if you talked it over it might help you out."

"Well," he said, "I s'pose it wouldn't hurt." And he started to cry.

"I'm gonna have a funeral before Sunday. Tomorrow, and I think it's myself or my wife."

I said, "Gene, that's impossible. You're talking to me and if you dropped dead right now, it's Friday morning—we'd have to get a casket and get you ready."

At that time they had no funerals on Sunday so I said, "You wouldn't be ready before Monday.

"By jove, I never thought of that. It's gotta be the wife."

I said, "She's in the same boat that you're in. She couldn't be buried before Monday."

He said, "I saw the casket leave the door here and go all the way up to the church and a fairly nice crowd gathered."

I saw there was no use arguing with him so I spoke with him for a while, then I left.

When I got up to the house, the housekeeper told me that I was to call Father Johnstone, in Waterford.

I called and he informed me that a fellow, who was formerly from Long Island, had died in Waterford the night before and his final wish was that he be buried in Boisdale. Could I get some people to dig the grave and they would ship the remains up on the train, in the morning, and I could have a Mass at ten o'clock and have the funeral.

I called a few fellows to come and dig the grave and I thought of Gene. I went down to the station and said, "Gene, you're right. I'm gonna have a funeral tomorrow."

"Who in the hell is it?"

I told him who it was and he said, "Oh my God, it's time for him to die. I was thinkin' after you left, it wasn't me anyways. I was the last one in the procession!"

So, they sent the remains up but they took them into the station and took the casket out of the rough box and went out through Gene's front door and walked to the church.

D1825.7.1. Person sees phantom funeral procession some time before the actual procession takes place

121.

Before I went to college I was staying with my granduncle. One day I came down to Inverness, about five mile, and did some shopping and hung around until it was late afternoon. It was the fall of the year and it got dark about five o'clock. I came home and just put the wagon in on the thrashing floor and put the horse in the barn with the harness off. I was going to come and give him a drink when I got a bite to eat and got a little cooler. I went home and changed my clothes and a bit later went back to the barn. I went into the horse stable and I could see right through to the thrashing floor. God, here was a nice bulb of light on the seat of the wagon. And I had to go in there.

I let the horses out and cleaned the stables and the light was still there. I went over to the other side, let the cows out, looked through and the same light, on the seat of the wagon. Well, I had to go in and knock the hay down and feed them. As soon as I went into the thrashing floor, the light disappeared. I went up to get the hay, looked down, the light was in the wagon again. Well, I threw the hay down and, you can rest assured, I didn't waste much time serving the hay. I just threw it in the stalls and fed them and, on the floor, I wasn't seeing it.

I went to the house and didn't say a word to my granduncle because he was sick at the time. I thought it was a forerunner of some kind.

Three or four days later one of the neighbours came over. They were going to Inverness and they wanted to borrow the wagon. I gave them the wagon and they came back in the evening. We were talkin' at the barn for a while and the neighbour said, "I gotta tell you this. I had a queer experience today. Did you ever see any lights or anything on the wagon?"

I said, "Well, yes, I did," and I told him my story.

He said, "Well, I was going to Inverness and, at the Corner, met a hearse that had broken down. When I came along, they asked me if I would take the baby's remains from there to the cemetery. I took it and put it on the seat alongside of me."

That was the light I saw a few days before. And that happened.

E530.1.7. Ghost light indicates route funeral will take

122.

In April 1963, I was appointed dean of South Inverness. After I got my appointment I decided to have a meeting with all the priests. My first meeting. I went to bed around ten o'clock and I woke around two o'clock, because of a dream.

My dream was that President Kennedy had died. I saw the casket, I saw the room in which it was, I saw the flag draped over the casket and the four sailors, one standing at each corner. It kind of scared me so I maybe read or said a prayer or had a smoke and went back to sleep again.

The second time I had the dream, I was saying Mass for President Kennedy in the church in Port Hawkesbury. I was celebrant. We went through the Mass and came down to the false casket to say the prayers. I went around the casket with the holy water, in the dream, then I genuflected and took the censer. I said, "Where's the incense?" I was in a strange parish so I said to the pastor, "What'll I do?"

He said, "Finish up the prayer, genuflect and go in." Which is what we did, in the dream.

That woke me and I turned on the radio to see if there was anything on the news. There was not a thing.

The next day we had the deanery meeting and I told the priests, during lunch, the queer dream I had. "I think something's gonna happen to Kennedy."

They pooh-hooed me and the whole thing.

In November of '63 Kennedy was shot. On the night of the fatal event I stayed up until I saw the casket being taken off the airplane, in Washington, and I fell asleep.

Next morning I got up and turned on the news and they were showing the casket and it was identical to the dream I had. I could see the drapes around the wall. I could see the casket, closed, and the flag over it and the four sailors, one at each corner.

In the evening a phone call came. The bishop had asked the deans to contact all the priests in the deanery and tell them to say Mass for President Kennedy, the day of the funeral, at a time suitable to all the people. So, I did that and the priests all agreed.

Then the phone rang again and it was the pastor in Hawkesbury and he asked would I mind saying two Masses that day. I said, "There are quite a few working at the mill from my parish and from your parish and Judique and Creignish and West Bay Road."

He said, "If we had Mass at seven we could satisfy all. We'll have a solemn High Mass."

I said, "Sure."

So, I went in the day of the funeral and the pastor said, "You say the Mass, I'll go deacon, and the curate'll go sub-deacon."

We went through the Mass, came down for the prayers at the false casket. I said the prayers, I sprinkled the casket and I came around and took the censer. No incense. I said, "What'll I do now? What about the incense?"

The pastor said, "Forget about it. Finish off the prayers, we'll genuflect and go in the vestry." Which is what we did.

D1812.3.3.11 Death of another revealed in dream

D1813.1. Dream shows events in distant place

123.

I've seen myself, on a number of occasions, close the church, lock the church, put all the lights out and come down to the house. Then, a last look at the church before I'd go into the office, and the church would be all lit up. Every light on.

I'd turn around and go back up. I'd go in the little porch outside the vestry, unlock the door, open it and everything was in darkness. I'd switch all the lights on and go around the church looking to see if there was anybody there. I'd even call out. Nothing.

I'd put the lights out, lock the door and go back to the house.

The church would remain in darkness.

But within a week or two weeks at the most we'd have a wake in the church.

E530.1.0.1(c). Building seen to light up strangely at night when unoccupied

E530.1.6. Ghost light serves as death omen

ARCHIE NEIL CHISHOLM

MARGAREE FORKS

124.

They used to tell about this group that used to go to a particular church. Whether it was Catholic or Protestant makes no difference but the clergyman always insisted, about every two or three months, that they'd stand up in church and profess themselves as to whether they had sinned greatly or not. They didn't have to tell their sins but some of them would.

There was this one particular lady, she had never been married but she was about fifty or fifty-five. On this occasion, she got up and she made quite a do about a sin that she had committed. That she'd had this affair and all this, and she made quite a long story. Finally, she sat down and that was all right.

Two or three months afterwards, he called on all those sinners to get up and to confess that they had been sinners. Up she got again and she told about her affair with this particular man and it was the same story over again.

This finally happened about four times till, at last, the clergyman involved got sick and tired of listening to her, and he took her to one side and he said, "Now, you confessed your misdemeanor, that you had sinned. You confessed the same thing four times, of having this affair with this man. I don't think there's any call for you to do this again."

"Aw," she said. "Yes, Father, but I so love to talk about it!"

J1260. Repartee based on church or clergy
J2350. Talkative fools **V20. Confession of sins**

125.

A fellow was very much in love with his wife and they had spent, probably, twenty years together and lived a very, very happy life. But he died quite suddenly and she was still extremely good-looking. She lived on for twenty, twenty-five years, and she died and she went up to heaven.

When she met St. Peter, she asked him if he could tell her where Willy MacDonald lived. Well, St. Peter looked at the book and he said, "There are eleven thousand, nine hundred and seventy-eight Willy MacDonalds that I have listed here. Was there any distinguishing mark about him that you could tell?"

"Well, no."

"Did he ever say anything to you that would indicate where I could find him?"

She said, "Well, no. The last thing he told me, just before he died, was that if I ever kissed a man after he died that he would turn over in his grave."

St. Peter says, "You needn't look any farther. We call him Whirling Willy up here!"

E561. Dead person spins
F11. Journey to heaven (upper-world, paradise)
F403.2.3.5. Familiar spirit reveals infidelity of man's wife
X700. Humour concerning sex

126.

I give you a story that I can prove, with ample proof, of three fellows who left Middle River. One fellow's name was Angus MacDonald, and Mose Murphy from Northeast Margaree, and my brother Dan, who's dead now.

Danny was working at MacRae's, in Middle River, and this Angus MacDonald bought a new car. Now, this wasn't yesterday. It was a new McLaughlin Buick. It was a soft-topped car.

They were driving around on a Sunday afternoon, through Margaree Forks, and they were probably all feeling pretty good at the time.

My brother was supposed to go back to Middle River with them and, when he came to the store at Margaree Forks, he got them to stop and he got out and he cooked up some excuse that he wasn't going back to Middle River with them.

They had a third man with them from Northeast Margaree and he was in the front seat. Now, the emergency brakes on these old Buicks was right in the center of the car, on the floor.

Danny got out of the car and hung around, for no particular reason in the world, and they took off. They hadn't gone four miles when, right at the turn where you go up the hill to Sydney, at Northeast Margaree—this fellow was doing sixty miles an hour, which would be nothing today but, on the old narrow roads, that was a tremendous speed—and the guy that was with them got terrified and he grabbed the emergency brake and hauled it on. The car upended, Mose Murphy was killed, MacDonald was killed, MacKenzie escaped—and my brother escaped by not being in that car. He got out only about ten minutes before and he could never explain the reason why.

D1812.0.1. Foreknowledge of hour of death

D1812.4. Future revealed by presentiment

127.

There was a certain boy from Margaree who was a very heavy drinker. He was a great deal of worry to his parents. He'd come home at all hours of the night, loaded. His father died and it didn't seem to change him very much.

This night, quite a stormy night in the winter, he got out of a car and the front door of his house was locked. His two brothers were sitting in the living room. One of them came to the door and opened it. He says, "John, who was with you when I opened the door?"

John was half cut and he says, "There was nobody with me at all."

"Yes, there was," and he described a man with this long overcoat and the heavy dark cap. He described their father to perfection.

Well, John thought that this was a story made up to sort of scare him off the booze and he didn't pay too much attention to it.

Another night, John was out on the prowl again. He and his friend came home, to Margaree Forks, and it was very stormy. John was extremely full and he fell in a snow bank and he wasn't getting up from there.

The house was in darkness, they were all in bed. All of a sudden, one of John's brothers jumped out of bed and he pulled on his boots and his coat. His wife said to him, "Where in the name of God are you going?"

He said, "John is outside in the snow bank and he'll freeze to death if I don't take him in."

He went out and he took John in and straightened him out some.

The next day he was telling John about it. John said, "What puzzles me is how did you know I was there?"

The brother said, "Our father—whether I was asleep or awake I don't know—but he appeared to me, in the bedroom, and told me to go out and get you."

E327.4. Ghost of father returns to rebuke child

E363.3. Ghost warns the living

128.

I asked Hector Doink one time about his experiences when he was out West, and he told me how bad the cold was compared to Cape Breton. He said we think it's cold here, but he was working forty miles north of The

Pas. They'd get their mail at a waystation and the mailbag that was going out would be on a hook and there was like an arm would come out, according to Hector, from the train. It would drop one bag and pick the other one off the hook.

They were in the middle of the winter, during the Depression years, and none of them had very heavy clothing so they were freezing. Hector said they sent down to Ottawa for warm clothing and, instead of sending them clothing, the government sent them about a half a carload of mailbags.

The mailbags were wind proof so each one cut the bags up and made kind of a suit for himself.

Hector said it was his turn to go in this day, for the mail. The train came along, snapped the arm out and, instead of snapping the mailbag, it snapped him and he found himself in a mailbox, 170 miles north of The Pas, in Manitoba.

X1620. Lies about cold weather

X1750. Absurd disregard of the nature of objects

129.

A fellow that was a native of Margaree was fishing on the river and you could never get him away from the river. Everybody used to talk about him, the way he'd stick to the river at all times.

This stranger from New York happened to come along with his fishing rod. Now, it's courtesy on the river to let whoever is ahead of you keep on down the pool and you follow him down. You never go ahead of them.

So this stranger was following the native down, fishing salmon, and they noticed a funeral coming. Very suddenly, the native of Margaree dropped his fishing rod, took his hat and held it over his heart, and he bowed with great respect and blessed himself as the funeral was going by.

This was a totally new thing to the fellow from New York. He didn't know what it was all about. When the funeral was gone by and the fellow resumed his fishing, the fellow from New York said to him, "Why did you take your hat off and bless yourself when the funeral was going by?"

The avid fisherman looked at him and said, "Well, rest her soul, I couldn't do anything less. That was my wife's funeral."

J1540. Retorts between husband and wife

T230. Faithlessness in marriage **T271. The neglected wife**

Dan Angus Beaton

BLACKSTONE

130.

Many, many years ago, back in Scotland, there was a voice in a graveyard calling for a man by the name of Ranald Young Allan.

Nobody in the area lived by that name and this voice was calling in the graveyard for approximately two hundred years, which is an awful long time.

There was a family and they were MacLeods and, by golly, young Allan got married and his first-born son was sent to be baptized. One of the neighbours came to the house, an older man, to see the newborn baby that was in the community. He asked them if the baby was in and they said, "No, the baby's on its way to the church to be baptized."

"Well, what did you call him?"

"We're calling him Ranald."

"My gracious!" he says. "Don't you people realize that that is the man that the voice has been calling, for over two hundred years, in the graveyard?"

And the father jumped up and says, "I never thought of it. I must catch up with the party that went with the baby to be baptized, before they get to the church and stop that baptism and call him another name."

But, fast as he could go, he still didn't catch up. When he got to the church, the baby was baptized and called Ranald.

Anyway, the father took it so bad that he moved from where he was, in Scotland, in the Isle of Skye. He went close to the border of England, clear across Scotland altogether, so the son would never know of him being called for in this graveyard.

Well, the son was growing up and he was a very big, strong man and he went working on a sailboat. Through having a fair education and being a good, strong labour man, he was no time on the boat when he became captain.

He had never heard of this voice calling for him but there was one old fellow with him that knew of it, but he never told him. Well, this trip that he was on, there came a terrible storm and he said to the crew, "We have to go into this harbour for shelter."

That was it, they went in, and the first thing he heard after they dropped anchor was the calling for Ranald Young Allan to come to where he was.

He turned to the crew and he said, "Who in the name of fortune would know that I came into this harbour?"

This old fellow told him. He says, "This voice has been calling for you, from a graveyard, many, many years before you were born. So, whatever you do, don't go there."

He says, "Well, if the man has been calling for me from before I was born, he must need me desperately bad. We'll have to go there."

He appointed six of the fellows to lower the boat and go with him. As they lowered the boat, the voice called for Ranald Young Allan to come alone and to take his sword.

He said, "Well, if he needs me bad enough to kill me, I'm going. I'm going to go to see what that person wants."

He jumped in the boat, alone, and rowed ashore and he took his sword as the voice told him. He had to travel about four miles before he got to the graveyard and, as he was traveling through the brush, he was getting closer and closer to the voice. At long last, he came to the grave and here was the man, sticking out of the grave, halfway up.

He walked over and the man said, "At long last you have come."

Ranald asked him, "Why, in the name of fortune, should you

be calling for me for so long?"

He says, "I knew that you'd be the only man that would ever have the courage to come in here and do what I want done."

Ranald said, "What is it you want done so badly?"

He says, "When I was a young man, I promised a certain girl that I'd marry her, regardless of what happened. Even if I lost the head from my shoulders. I didn't keep that promise and there's no rest for me, in the hereafter, until that promise is fulfilled. When you cut my head off, leave the sword lay on my neck until the blood gets cold. Then the task will be completed."

Ranald says, "That I'll do for you." And he took the sword and, with one swing, the head came right off him. And he left the sword on the neck until the blood was cold, and everything disappeared. The voice was never heard after.

And that's the story as it was told to me.

D1420.4. Helper summoned by calling his name
E411.0.2.1. Return from dead to do penance
E417. Dead person speaks from grave
E431.7.2. Decapitating in order to prevent return
Q266. Punishment for breaking promise

131.

The story I'm gonna tell you people now, well, you'll have to make up your own mind as to what it is. It's called The Red Thread.

I was about twelve years old, my father was working on the railroad and, in those days, the cart was the most useful implement on a farm and, of course, they had to be kept in shape. We had to take the cart wheels to the forge to have new hubs put in and spokes put in.

Him and I left and we got there and they told us at the forge, "You'll have to leave your work here. We cannot do this now. If you'll be here a week from this evening, the cart wheels will be ready."

That was all right. We left the wheels there and we went back home. The following week, just on that same day, I again had my uncle's cart down and ready to go for the wheels. We went, and we went to the forge and, when we got there, they were working on the wheels. They weren't yet completed and they had about another hour's work to do on the wheels. The men told my father and I, "You fellows go in the house and the women'll make you tea, until we're through."

So we did. Went in the house and there was a real old lady, oh, up in her 90s, sitting at the end of the table, knitting. My father and the old lady got talking and she told him that she come over from Scotland when she was a young girl, when she was about seven years of age. So, the conversation was going on.

Then she said, "My, my, we had a terrible loss here this morning."

My father said, "Now, what might that loss be?"

"Well, you know, we had a beautiful steer in the barn and when the men went out this morning, the steer was dead. It was to be our fall and winter's meat and now we haven't any."

My father said, "That's quite a loss. What happened to him? Did he hang himself with the rope that was tying him?"

"Oh, indeed, no," she said. "He never had a rope around his neck. He was in a box stall."

Then my father said, "Must have been some other sickness."

"He wasn't sick either," she said.

"Well, something happened that killed him."

"Ha, haa, I know," the old lady said. "But if I thought it was Black John over there that did that to us, I'd put the red thread to work and there wouldn't be an animal alive on his farm tomorrow."

My father said to her, "Those are pretty strong words. Would that be possible?"

"Oh, indeed, it would be possible," she said. "And many is the time I put the red thread to work. I'll tell you and you can look into the matter for yourself.

"Just about a year ago was the last time I put the red thread to work. There was a fellow here with wheels, the same as you are, and he was from the Inverness area. The wheels wasn't ready and he come in and he had tea and he was awful cross about it. In fact, he was very dirty about the wheels not being ready as they were promised. But one of the men working was sick for three or four days and that's why his wheels wasn't ready.

"However," she said, "after we had treated him good, he was goin' out the door and the dog was lying down right alongside the door. When he went out, he hauled off and he gave the dog an awful dirty kick. Indeed, it made me so mad that I put the red thread to work. And that foot that kicked the dog certainly wouldn't kick him the next morning because it was darn well broken for him."

My father made it his business—he knew the man—and the next time he was in town he went to see him. He never told him anything about the old lady. He said, "I heard you had your leg broken."

"Indeed it was," he said.

"Well, what happened?"

"Well, I was away at the forge last year, and when I come home, we had a big, brown horse—a quiet animal that never raised a foot in his life. And when I was hanging the harness behind him he kicked me! He broke my leg between the hip and the knee. Doctor MacMaster was in Inverness at that time and he said that my leg was so bad that they had to send me to Antigonish. I was two months in Antigonish before I got home. I'm only just gettin' it started to walk on it."

D1184. Magic thread
G263.4.3 Witch cripples or lames through illness
G265.4.1. Witch causes death of animals
Q285.1. Cruelty to animals punished

132.

Ronald Rankin, from Black River, was a great friend of the family and he was road foreman in that area for a number of years. Of course he had the road patronage and, in the Depression years believe you me, if you got a couple of days work on the road, with a team or something like this, oh, you'd be a lucky person.

However, this time, one of the girls spoke and said, "Ronald Rankin is coming to the house."

I said, "That's fine."

And Ronald came in and sat down and I asked him how he was and he said, "Fine." Then Ronald Rankin turned around and he says, "Look, Dan Angus, I came here on purpose to see you today. I want to find out from you what you and I were doing up the Broad Cove Banks, in a field, last night. About eleven o'clock at night."

Well, great glory, I was home and in bed at eleven o'clock. I turned around and I looked at Ronald. I was wondering if he was going astray in the mind.

"You and I were seen in that field, last night, and I am wondering what we were doing there."

I said, "Ronald, it couldn't have been me that was with you because I wasn't anywhere near Broad Cove Banks last night. "

He says, "I know and neither was I, but you'll be there and I'll be with you! And to prove my story will be true, when we're there, a third man'll come along that shouldn't be with us at all."

And Ronald left me like that.

Time was going by and finally, who died but old Johnson. He used to be mine manager in Inverness and Eddie Smith was married to his daughter.

Okay. He was waked at Eddie's. Mrs. Eddie Smith asked me if I'd be one of the pallbearers for her father and I said, "Yes, willingly." And she asked Ronald Rankin if he'd be a pallbearer for her father and he said yes. Fine.

The morning of the funeral the hearse pulled up and the remains were put in the hearse and we left with the remains. I took the car and Ronald Rankin went with me. We drove right along and they turned up the Banks road, with the remains.

Something I didn't know, that there was a graveyard somewheres close to the shore. An old Presbyterian graveyard down there. And when Johnson came over, early in 1900, he had a little daughter that died and there's where she was buried. He asked to be buried in the same graveyard with his daughter.

When we got that far up with the remains, the remains were

shifted and there was a horse, with an express wagon, waiting in that field, and the remains were shifted into the express wagon. We hadda walk quite a distance, a long distance we had to go, and Ronald Rankin, I knew, had a bad heart condition. Ronald had never thought of it, when we were in that field, but we didn't go a hundred feet, walking behind the casket, when I said to myself, "Here's where I was seen with Ronald Rankin and, sure as fate, somethin's gonna happen."

And my first thought was that Ronald Rankin was going to take a heart attack and possibly die. You understand? But, by golly, nothing was happening. We were walking along and, when we were quite a ways in the field, who came along but this third person, whose name I'm not going to give, loaded down with bush whiskey. A great friend of Ronald's and a fairly good friend of my own. And his buddy was waiting out at the road with the result that, when we got Johnson down to the graveyard—it's customary for the pallbearers to put some of the dirt on the casket, fill the grave—we didn't get to do that chore because this fellow was with us. We had to leave some of the rest do this and take this fellow out to the road.

Just as Ronald had told me, five or six months before that. He joined his buddies and I went home.

And they'll tell you that there are no forerunners! But there are forerunners, as sure as fate.

D1825.7.1. Person sees phantom funeral procession some time before the actual procession takes place

133.

The person involved in this story was born in Black River, in 1871. His name is Ronald Beaton. He was ordained in 1902, in Rome, and he returned home and spent several years in the diocese of Antigonish. Then, he transferred to the West.

On this certain day, he was returning back home from the mission church to the mother church, so to speak, and he got caught in an awful prairie storm. Just about dusk, in the middle of that storm, he noticed a little light and he figured, where there was light there was shelter. When he got there, it was a little shack on the prairie. A woman came to the door and she told him, "You cannot come in till I ask my husband if it's all right."

She asked her husband, "There's a Catholic priest at the door. Will let him in?"

Her husband answered, "Let the dog in. It's not fit for the devil himself out tonight but he'll be out of here at daylight in the morning."

Well then, she let him in and he sat down on this here block of wood while the woman of the house was busying herself, making supper for her husband. Father Ronald asked her, "Are you a Canadian? Were you born in Canada?"

"Oh, yes," she says. "I was born in Canada."

He says, "What part of Canada did you come from?"

She says, "Well, I came from the province of Nova Scotia."

"Well, well," he said to her. "What part of the province of Nova Scotia did you come from?"

She says, "I came from Cape Breton Island."

"Well lady, we're gettin' close to home. So did I come from Cape Breton Island. What part of Cape Breton did you happen to come from?"

She said, "I came from Cape Mabou. Do you know where that is?"

"Indeed I do," he said. "Whose daughter would you be, from Cape Mabou?"

She named the MacLean family she was from. She was a MacLean.

"Well, well," he said. "Lady, how often I carried the mail bag from Black River, across your home, just to the post office."

"And who, in the name of fortune, are you?" she said.

He said, "I'm Ronald Beaton, Big Finlay Beaton's son, from Black River."

And she knew Big Finlay Beaton and his people very well.

Well, while he was talking to her and while she was busy making supper, he could hear someone groaning, in a little room back of the stove. He never said a word. Finally, she turned around and she said to her husband, "Frank, this man came from the very place that I came from. He knows all my people and I know his people. Would it be all right for me if I gave him some supper?"

"By all means, if you know him, give him some supper."

So things were getting a little more friendly.

After they had supper, he turned around and he asked her, "Is there anyone else in this house besides the two of you?"

"Yes," she said. "There's an old lady, my husband's step-mother, in the room down there."

He says, "I thought I heard someone groaning or moaning down there. Could I see her?"

She said, "Oh, it wouldn't do you any good to go down and talk to her. She hardly speaks any English at all, only Polish."

"Well," he said, "I am fluent in eleven languages"—which he was—"and I am very fluent in Polish."

"In that case, perhaps it would help if you did go down and see her."

So, he went down and here she was in the bed. He spoke to her in Polish and she looked at him and she just seemed to come to life.

"My God," she said, and here she had the rosary tied in her hand. "You wouldn't by any means be a Catholic priest?"

He said, "Yes, I am."

She said, "Well, I'm bedridden for over twenty years and I been praying night and day that I'd die with the last rites of the church. Will you anoint me and prepare me for death?"

And he said, "I'll do that, gladly."

Nobody objected and, when he was all through, he was talking to her, in Polish, and she just really enjoyed that.

Early in the morning, the woman of the house was up, and in the old wood stove she made a fire. She made a cup of tea for the old lady who was down in the room. She went down and when she went down, she screamed. She came back and she hollered at Frank, "My God, the old lady is dead!"

Frank got up and, of course, Father Ronald got up. The man of the house said, "I'll have to go to town, get some boards and some nails and make a box to put the old lady in. Then, dig a hole, in back of the barn and bury her."

Father Ronald said to him, "Now, if you're going into town, I'll get into town with you."

"That'll be fine. You can ride along with me."

Ronald said, "You make the box, put the old lady in it, but don't bury her back of the barn. Don't dig a grave for her at all. You take her to our church and I'll get parishioners to dig a grave, in the graveyard. And I'll see that she'll be properly buried there."

He said, "Well, that'd be a lot easier for me and I'll do that."

Father Ronald says, "Now tomorrow, when you bring the remains in, be sure and come into the house and I'll see that you get your dinner and you'll be well looked after."

The next day, they landed with the remains and the priest had parishioners dig a grave in the graveyard, and he buried her with the last rites of the church.

After that, the priest told them when they were leaving, "Whenever you're in here, be sure and visit me. You can have a cup of tea or a hot meal."

So, the old lady received the last rites before she died and the last rites for the graveyard. And the eventual thing was they became great friends and they also became parishioners of that parish.

And that's what I call the power of prayer.

V20. Confession of sins

V52. Miraculous power of prayer **V60. Funeral rites**

V331.10.1. Conversion to Christianity through forgiveness and gentleness

134.

This one I know is true or I wouldn't be telling it at all. I know the people. I know it was my father and mother.

They went to a party, not too far from their own home, and it was in the heart of the winter. It was years ago.

Rather than go by sleigh, they went through the fields and he said to my mother—and they were relatively young—he said, "I'll put the new blanket on the horse, and we'll jump on horseback and ride through the fields to where the party is."

They were going by one of the neighbour's houses [John and Mary's], where the woman had died the summer before. On their way back, about two o'clock in the morning, they were coming by this house. My mother looked and she saw the woman that had died, coming in from the well with two pails of water and she said to my father, "Finlay, for God's sake, look at Mary coming in with two pails of water, from the well. Stop the horse at once. I'm going to talk to her."

My father was the most kindly person in the world. My father just wrapped the reins around the horse and took off as fast as he could gallop. No way was he stopping!

[A fellow] came to my father and mother's place and they gave him the full story. My father and mother told him the whole story.

"All right," he says. "I'll stay at John's place tonight."

He went there and he stayed there that night. He sat right at the window, at the table, praying with his prayer book. Shortly after nine o'clock, he was looking out the window. "John," he says, "she's out there. Go out and talk to your wife."

The fellow slowly got up and he went out. He was out about ten minutes, talking to his wife.

Now, she died in childbirth, so his children were all small. And she had borrowed two blankets. In them days, there were no hospitals and it was only midwives and she had borrowed the blankets from one of the neighbour women, and the woman she borrowed them from would never tell the husband because she just wouldn't want to interfere.

His wife told him, "I won't be resting in the other world until those blankets are returned. I borrowed them for the purpose of the baby's birth. The blankets have to be returned. You go and get the neighbour's woman and she'll know her own blankets. When the blankets are returned, I'll be at rest in the other world."

And that's all that had to be done. The blankets were returned and all was addressed.

And she wasn't the only one that my mother saw. She saw different ones.

E322. Dead wife's friendly return

E340. Return from dead to repay obligation

135.

We all speak of ghosts of people who are dead. I'm gonna tell you, I've had experience with ghosts and this is true. I'm not lying to you. Don't ever be afraid of a ghost of a dead person. But, if you see the ghost of a live person, then you'd better be worried. This is true.

This story I'm going to tell you now happened right in the Blackstone area about 1895—between 1890 and 1895. It was my uncle and my aunt. They went to a dance in the neighbourhood and, in those days, they walked there. They're both dead now. And there was a fellow at the dance that insisted he was going to take my aunt home from the dance. No way! She didn't want any part of him and he was pretty sore about it.

So they decided, my uncle and aunt, they'd leave for home rather early. The dance was still going on. They had, perhaps, a mile and a half or perhaps two miles to walk. When they were about halfway home, this black thing tried to swipe her right off her feet and take her with him.

She screamed and she hollered and my uncle grabbed her. She didn't know what it was but he saw and knew what it was. And this thing went right by, in the form of a man.

John reached in and pulled a stake right out of the fence that was alongside the road. When it came back and tried to grab her again, he laid him right with the stake. All was over.

At that very instant, that very same fellow that insisted he was going to take her home, was flattened as flat as a pancake, right in the dance hall, and the people didn't know, in the name of God, what had happened to the man.

And that story is as true as we're sittin' here!

E461. Fight of revenant with living person

E722.1.2. Soul as black or white entity

E723.4. Wraith does what person wishes to do but is unable to do in the flesh

136.

I'm gonna tell you people tonight a story that happened in 1918. I was fifteen years of age.

Centreville is approximately thirteen miles, around the road, from where I lived but, by crossing through farms, fields and the woods, I could shorten it to about eight miles.

So I started off, but the sky was darkening over awful fast. The night was closing in fast. At last, the big crash of thunder came and the lightning and the rain started pouring down.

On my path home I had to cross by a vacant house, so I made for the vacant house. I wondered if I could get in there. Sure enough, I could open the latch on the door and I got in. I started up the stairway. I wondered if there was an old bed somewheres that I could lie down in. When I got at the head of the stairs I could see, to my right, a window in the end of the house. And I could see a door that was open there. Sure enough, there was an old wooden bed in there.

I wasn't too long there when I started hearing this soft thump. Some kind of a soft thump. I started wondering what that could be. I wasn't too scared of ghosts. I thought as long as it was down below and I was up above, it wasn't too bad. But it started getting louder and louder.

Eventually, I heard as if somebody was tearing cloth. I said to myself, "The wind wouldn't be doing that." Hearing this cloth being torn.

Finally, I heard walking down below. Well, I'm going to be truthful and tell you the real truth. I was scared then and I took to praying. I was never very good at praying but I was praying my best then.

After a while, the steps started coming up the stairs. The closer they were coming to the head of the stairs, the more scared I was getting, mister.

Be that as it may, the steps got to the head of the stairs. Well, my only wish in my heart—and I could hear my heart hitting right inside my chest—was that them steps would go off the other way. But no such luck. The steps started right over towards the bedroom where I was, on the bed.

Finally, the lightning showed up again and the form of a woman was standing at the foot of the bed. I shiver yet when I think of it. Some way or another, something caused me to say, "In the name of God, who are you and where did you come from?"

Once I spoke, I could see her ever so much plainer. "Oh," she said, "I'm so glad that you spoke to me. It's a godsend that you're here."

I said, "Who are you? Are you of this world?"

She said to me, "I was once but I'm not now."

I said to her, "What do you want with me?"

"There's a lot I want you to do for me. If you'll follow me, I'll not only tell you but show you what I want done."

I said, "All right," and immediately she seemed to have a kind of a lamp with a chain on it and a light only out of the bottom of it. A light that made a circle. Not a bright light, a dull light.

First thing I know, I found myself following her. When we got to the foot of the stairs, she turned to the left. We went in to what I figure was the old kitchen and there the light shone on an old cellar hatch with a steel ring in it. She asked me if I'd be good enough to open the hatch, the cellar hatch.

I'm telling you right now, I didn't know what was going to happen when I'd open the cellar hatch, but I had no choice. I reached out and I opened the hatch and I leaned it against the wall. She said, "Now, you can follow me."

And she went down and I noticed she never stood on a step at all. But there was an old ladder going down to the cellar and I went down on that.

She turned to the right and she walked over toward an old cellar wall and, just as we got close, there was a sliver of wood on the floor and she asked me to pick it up. I picked it up and she went over and she pointed her finger to the ground and asked me, "Will you make the sign of the cross?"

I said yes and I put the sign of the cross there.

She said, "Now, leave the stick in the center of it."

I pushed the little stick in the ground, and here's where her story comes in.

She turned around and she told me, "I was living here with my father, alone, and my father was very sick. In the spring of the year he wanted me to hire a young person, who was in the neighbourhood, to make the fences and plant the potatoes and put in other crops.

"This I did and we became very close friends, this young man and I, with the result that I became pregnant. In the fall of the year I told him of my situation. The next week, without me knowing anything, he left the country.

"In the middle of February a little girl was born to me, in an awful snowstorm. Nobody in the house but myself and my father, who was bedridden and he didn't know my situation. The morning the baby was born I could see she wasn't very strong. She lived only a short time after I'd baptized her.

"I kept her in bed with me for a day before I wrapped her up in a sheet that I had torn up and put her down in the lower end of the house, which was very cold. I left her there for two weeks until something had to be done. So, I buried her where that little cross is.

"What I want you to do is to take this story to the priest of my parish and he will show you a spot in the graveyard where I want you to take those little remains and have them buried in consecrated ground. When she's buried the priest will bless the little grave, and my troubles and hers will be complete."

I said, "I'll do that."

We went up from the cellar and I could see that daylight was just beginning to break. As we walked towards the door, I was alone. There was nobody there but me. I started off then home. The rain had stopped, the lightning was over.

That Sunday morning I asked my father if it'd be all right for me to go to the other parish church, no more than a mile further than our own church. He said, "Whatever church you go to is all right with me, but go to church."

So I jumped on horseback and I rode to church. When Mass was over I waited and I went in and I saw this priest that she wanted me to see. I told him the whole story. He says, "You wait. You'll have dinner with me and you and I'll go to the graveyard and I'll show you where that little girl will be buried."

This was done and the next morning, at two o'clock, I left with the team from home and I went to this old vacant house. I dug up the remains in the cellar and I was in the graveyard just when day was breaking. I did what she had asked me to.

And that story is as true as the gospel of the church.

E323.5. Mother returns to search for dead child

E338.1. Non-malevolent ghost haunts house or castle

E412.2.2. Mother of unbaptized child cannot rest in grave

E412.3. Dead without proper funeral rites cannot rest

E419.8. Ghost returns to enforce its burial wishes or to protest disregard of them T640. Illegitimate children

137.

Old John MacIsaac, he was a carpenter, went to this place to work. There was rumours that the place was haunted, and John was scared of his own shadow. However, he figured as long as the people were in the house with him he could get along all right.

But the first day he went to work it just so happened the family was going to a wedding that evening. The woman told him, "We'll have an early supper, Mr. MacIsaac, and if you want to you can make tea for yourself and you can go to bed anytime you want. Or you can wait up until we come home. Now I'll show you where your bedroom is."

She took him up to the room where he was to sleep and he noticed the clothes that was hanging in the bedroom and they looked like those of the man who had died there recently. He figured maybe that was the spook that was being seen. He also noticed high, leather boots at the head of the bed along with an overcoat and a derby hat hanging at the foot of the bed.

Came the hour of nine o'clock and he was still waiting up. Came ten and he decided he'd go up to his room and lie down on the bed. He turned the lamp down some and he was telling Alex Cameron the story.

"I wasn't in bed long when I was hearing a noise and I thought it was them coming home. But good God, what was it but the boots at the head of the bed backed out from the bed, walked out and started down the stairs! And as deaf as I was, I could hear every step going down and I made out that they went outside.

"My decision then was, what was I to do? Was I going to wait in this room until they came back or was I gonna make for outside where there was more room to run?

"I figured, by hell, it's too small to get away from him inside, if he'd come back, and I decided that if I could get out he'd have a hell of a job catching me.

"I too started down the stairs but, believe me, I was an awful frightened man. All I remember is this: when I got to the foot of the stairs and I was at the door, the clock started to strike twelve. By the time I got in home, two-and-a-half miles away, my clock was just finishing striking twelve."

E338.1. Non-malevolent ghost haunts house or castle

F823. Extraordinary shoes

J1495. Person runs from actual or supposed ghost

X1796.2*. Lie: running ability

ALEX JOHN MACISAAC

DUNVEGAN

138.

A number of years ago, I was running a lobster factory in Mabou Coal Mines. There was this old fellow there, an old fisherman, he fished lobsters and he fished herring, too. So one day, he got an oversized herring in the net. He thought that he'd keep it alive. He had a bucket in the boat so he put seawater in and then put the herring in.

He took the herring home and it got so used to jumping out of the bucket that he was getting along pretty good without being in the water. It used to follow him around to the barn and across here and there.

This certain day, the old fellow was going after the cows. The herring was coming behind him and they were going across a bridge, over the brook.

Didn't the herring fall in the brook and get drowned!

X1306.3*. Tragic end to tame fish

139.

Flora and Sarah, they were going to a picnic one time.

This is years ago and they never saw a bicycle. There wasn't many of them around at that time.

By God, they were walking to the picnic and they saw this young fellow coming on a bicycle. They were back and forth on the road. They didn't know what the heck was coming. Finally, the bicycle got up close to them and it hit Sarah. Knocked her right in the ditch. She didn't get hurt very bad and they made it to the picnic all right.

The next day, the neighbours were asking, "How was the picnic?"

Flora said, "Some picnic! That queer fella came along, with that rig that he had between his legs, on top of Sarah in the ditch of the road. That was the picnic we had!"

J1772. One object thought to be another

X700. Humour concerning sex

140.

There was an old fellow and

his sister, in the Rear somewheres, and the old fellow got sick. Old Doctor MacMaster was in Inverness, you remember, kind of a rough character, and he went up to see the old fellow. He saw the old woman was in there, and I guess he had to give this old fellow an enema. He was trying to get the old woman out of the room.

So, he did this and he did that and everything. She was sticking right in there.

Well, he thought that she'd go when he said, "While you're here, I've got to put kind of an operation on this old fellow."

That didn't put her out of the room at all.

He said, "Well, I never seen anything so God-darned tight as this."

The old woman said, "Wasn't all the MacInnises like that!"

J1430. Repartee concerning doctors and patients

141.

A neighbour of mine, he was ceilidhin' back of the Rear one night. And he was coming home about twelve o'clock at night. Just before he went in the house, he heard an awful racket over in the barn.

Well, he thought some of the cattle was loose so he went over. The cows were all laying down and there was nothing wrong with the horses, so he went back to the house.

About a year later, the next winter, his aunt died. She lived with them.

In them days they used to make the homemade coffins. I was making the coffin myself with some of them.

He sent the boys up after some boards that was in the barn. They got the boards and put them down. I went with them and, when we got down, the old fellow asked, "Anything happened when you were up in the Rear there?"

"Nothing happened," his son said. "But them darned old barn doors, that you put up on the beams, fell down on the floor."

"That's just the noise that I heard the night that I was coming from the ceilidh," the old man said.

D1827.1.2.3*. Sound of coffin-making in carpenter shop before order for coffin is received

142.

There was an old woman went to Chicago to see her daughter. She wasn't away very much in her life and she thought that she'd go to New York from there. She had some relatives there too. She went down to the station and said, "I want a ticket to New York."

"Would you like to go by Buffalo?"

"No, by train, you damn fool!"

J2450. Literal fool

WILFRED SAMPSON

ARICHAT

143.

This fellow from L'Ardoise used to jack deer, you know, and the Mountie was trying to catch him. He'd been after trying to catch him shooting deer at night.

There's an orchard between L'Ardoise and Grand River and, apparently, this fellow had his buddy drop him off at this abandoned farm. But the Mountie knew he was going there.

So, the Mountie had the other Mountie from St. Peters drop him off, and he hid in the woods, about six o'clock.

The other fellow came about seven o'clock.

Well, the Mountie waited and he was waiting. He had a gun and the light and, when it come on to dark, he sure enough heard a noise down there. The guy put on the light and the Mountie wasn't far from him. He come out from the bush where he was and he grabbed him by the shoulder and says, "I gottcha now! Gimme that light."

So he took the light off the young fellow.

The young fellow says, "Why didn't you come here two minutes later? Jehoshaphat, it's the biggest buck I ever seen in my life. I've never seen a big buck like that. Flash the light down there in those trees and you'll see it. You won't believe it! That's a giant!"

He said the Mountie up and shone the light and he up with the gun and shot the deer!

The Mountie was gonna take him in. The young guy says, "How?"

"Well, I'm gonna charge you," says the Mountie.

"Charge me!" he says. "Just think, you're gonna be the laughing stock of St. Peters, when you come out before the judge and you tell him you were holdin' the flashlight for me to shoot the deer!"

So the Mountie said, "You take the deer and you get outta here. But I'll be watching you from now on."

The guy took off with the deer.

K301. Master thief

K1600. Deceiver falls into own trap

144.

This fellow by the name of Remy,

he had a brother and they used to hang around together all the time. They were close, Remy and Sylvester.

The old man, he was a hard ticket. He was a sea captain and he was hard on the kids. He'd give them a licking for nothing at all. They looked the wrong way, he'd haul off and whop them one or two. Just on general principle.

Anyway, they had a farm, on a cape. They had about twelve or fifteen sheep and they had a big ram.

This was late in the fall. In the old days, they had no cold storage so they used to kill the animals when it was December, when it was cold. In December it was like a deep freeze outside and they'd leave it hanging.

It was before Christmas anyway and the old man says, "Remy and Sylvester, I'm gonna get wood today, and I want to see that ram killed and up on the tripod and skinned by the time I come back tonight."

They started chasing the ram in the morning, about eight o'clock, and that ram was going like hell. They couldn't catch him. So, they got tired and, by noon, they went home to dinner. Remy says to Sylvester, "What the hell are we gonna do? We gotta do one thing or the other. We gotta catch that ram or leave home, because when the old man comes back he's gonna tan our hides."

Sylvester says, "I know what we'll do. We have an old musket over here. We'll load the old musket and we'll go out and we'll kill the ram."

Remy said, "Oh, that's good, but the old musket, there's no hammer on it. The trigger won't go off."

"Well, we'll use a hammer, and we'll hit the percussion cap with the hammer. You hold the gun and I'll hit it with the hammer when you say ready," said Sylvester. "And we'll kill the ram."

They loaded the old musket. They rammed nails in it and pieces of glass and rocks. They rammed her down, put powder in it, and they went up in the field.

They crawled up to this log that was laying there. Here was a knoll and the ram was up on the knoll and the twelve sheep were right around the knoll. The ram was standing there, with his big horns, right on the knoll.

Sylvester said to Remy, "Okay, you take good aim and, when you're ready, let me know and I'll hit the percussion cap with the hammer."

Remy laid down there and took the musket and aimed her good. Right for the head of the ram. "Okay, Sylvester, hit the percussion cap now!"

He hit it.

The musket damned near killed them. When the smoke cleared, here's the twelve sheep, all dead around the knoll and the ram going up the field, "Baa, baa, baa."

They left home before the old man came because he would have killed them just like they did the twelve sheep.

They were gone three days before they came back home.

J2172. Short-sightedness in caring for livestock

X1122.2. Lie: person shoots many animals with one shot

145.

This is a true story and it was told to me by my grandfather. It happened in Isle Madame. In the old days there was a ferry used to go from Louisdale to D'Escousse, and there was another ferry in Petit-de-Grat that used to go to Petit-de-Grat Island.

My great-grandfather lived in the Rocky Bay area. There were only two families living there but a lot of people used to come fishing in the summer.

What happened was, one stormy night, January the 13th, there was a knock on the door. My great-grandmother went to the door and this big blond man with queer clothes on was there. It was a kind of shiny suit, not like the serge that most of their clothes were made from.

She asked him, in French, what did he want. He answered her in a language and she didn't know what it was. Well, they asked him in. It was a cold, blizzardy night so they took him in. They fed him, but he couldn't speak a word of English or French.

Other people came to the house but nobody could understand his language. They took him with them to see the ferryman, the one that went from Isle Madame to Cape Breton. He told my great-grandfather, "No, that man never came across on this ferry. I'm the only ferryman and I would know."

So, they went to the Petit-de-Grat ferry and they asked the ferryman there. He said, "No, I've never seen the man before."

Well, he stayed with them through the winter. He didn't do much except split some wood for them. And he wrote on some paper, like a letter, but they couldn't understand the writing.

In the spring, my great-grandfather took him with them in the boat, fishing. The stranger got violently seasick and they had to bring him back to shore.

He stayed with them for a year to the day. January 13th, there was a storm again. He put his clothes on, walked out and they never, ever heard of him or saw him again.

The island is only about two and a half to three miles long and about a mile wide. They searched the island from one end to the other and never found anything. He never crossed on the ferries.

Where did he come from and where did he go? They didn't know.

I had an aunt who was a nun. She was in France and she was in England. When she was in France she had this letter and she sent it to a university in Heidelberg, Germany. They looked at the letter and said there was no known language in the world they knew, like that. They said it looked like logical writing but it was no language they knew about.

When she moved to England, she sent it to Edinburgh University and they told her the same thing.

This is a true story my grandfather told me.

D1815. Magic knowledge of strange tongues

H976. Task performed by mysterious stranger

Greg Smith

SOUTHWEST MARGAREE AND PORT HAWKESBURY

146.

An old Coady fellow was telling me, down in Margaree one time, about an experience he had with a fellow from New York.

He said, "I was down fishing salmon one morning and I had two or three settin' on the bank. Right across the pool from me was the fella from New York and he'd been fishing since hours and hours. Never caught a thing."

Finally, the fellow came over and said, "How come you're gettin' the salmon and I'm not getting any?"

The Coady fella said, "Well, for one thing, I wasn't using flies."

What he had with him was a big can of worms, a hook and a bottle of moonshine.

He said, "Now, this is my secret, right here. You do what I tell you. You take the bottle of shine and you have a drink. Then, you take the worm and you dip it in the moonshine and you put him on the hook."

Well, the New Yorker did this and, when he cast out, the line was no sooner in the water when there was an awful big splash and scuffle. The water was boiling

In a few minutes, he had the salmon on the shore and the worm had that salmon right by the throat!

X1153. Lie: fish caught by remarkable trick

HECTOR DOINK MACDONALD

BROAD COVE

147.

"You often talk about Giant MacAskill. Did you ever see any of his people?"

John Alex said, "No, but he's an awful powerful man. I read about him."

I turned around and said, "I seen his sister in North River. She was a big woman. I went up at the house and I met a girl at the door and asked, 'Where's MacAskill's sister?'"

"She's over on the hill there. You can go over and you'll see her."

I went over and do you know what she was doing? Knitting a wire fence with two crowbars.

X940. Lie: remarkable strong man

148.

One time I was down to St. Rose, to see my uncle. I went down in the wintertime. I landed down my uncle's and my grandmother said, "Has your mother got any holy water?"

"I don't know," I said. "I don't know."

"We got a lot of holy water here."

They used to see the devil down St. Rose, one time.

She filled a bottle with holy water and I started home.

A moonlight night, up near Danny MacLellan's and Dan Angus Joe's, I seen a man walking up ahead. I drew alongside of him. I asked him, "Want a ride, Mac?"

"Yes."

He stepped in and, as he stepped in, he had a horse's hoof on him. Well, I got scared.

Then I turned around and I said, "Would you like a drink of booze?"

"Yes, I'll take a drink o' booze."

I took the bottle of holy water and I give it to him.

Well, Lord merciful, when he drank the holy water he took the robe and everything to the sky! Lost the robe.

When I went home MacArthur asked, "Where's the robe?"

I said, "In Hell. If you want it, go after it."

G303.4.5.3.1. Devil detected by his hooves

G303.16.7. Devil is chased by holy water

149.

When I was working in Corner Brook down there, my gumshoes got awful bad and my feet used to be wet. I had five dollars so I went up to a little store. There was a pretty girl there and she was talking to me.

"I want a pair o' gumshoes."

"I got the gumshoes," she says.

And I threw the five dollars.

"No, we don't take money here. You go down the shore here, to the wharf. Ask some o' them fishermen to give you a bag of fish and you'll get the gumshoes."

I went down. Well, they filled a big bag. Talk about heavy! Weigh about two hundred and fifty pounds!

I was staggering when I went in. I give her them. "Here's the fish."

She give me the gumshoes.

When I was going out she hollered, "Here. Come here."

She put her hand in a barrel and she gave me five smelts, for change.

X200. Humour dealing with tradesmen

Z47. Series of trick exchanges

ARCHIE NEIL CHISHOLM

MARGAREE FORKS

150.

Malcolm Chisholm was a first cousin of mine, some of you might remember when he was a doctor in New Waterford. He started his practise in Margaree when he came out of Dalhousie University. He had a small office down at a place called Widow Lord's.

His first case was an old man who lived out on the mountain back of Margaree. He had been hand-mowing, and somehow the scythe caught him below the knee. He had quite a little gash, and he got somebody to drive him down with the horse and buggy. The doctor stitched up his leg, about five stitches in it, and when the old man went to settle with him he said, "How much?" He was pretty tight-fisted, the old fella.

Doctor Malcolm says, "That's five dollars."

He looked at the doctor for a little while. He peeled off the five one-dollar bills and, as he was going out the door, he said, "Well,

Chisholm, I'd hate to have you make a suit for me!"

J1430. Repartee concerning doctors and patients

151.

This clergyman was very bitter against a certain group, and two of this group belonged to his own congregation. He swore that they would not be buried in consecrated ground.

These two fellows and four others were killed in a mine accident. This was in the early days of the Inverness mine. As sworn, the clergyman refused to allow them to be buried in consecrated ground. They were buried instead in another area all together.

On two or three occasions their caskets were pushed up out of the ground, as if the two were not resting in their graves.

Finally, when the clergyman passed on, his successor was told the story, and he had the two caskets and the remains brought in and buried in the consecrated ground. There was never any trouble after that.

I got the story from Martin Cameron, from Margaree Forks, who used to work in the mines. I was ten or eleven years of age when I heard him tell the story, repeatedly, to my father.

D1641.13. Coffin moves itself

E412.3. Dead without proper funeral rites cannot rest

152.

There were two brothers—long dead now—I'll call them Sandy and Alex. They would go to a picnic or a dance and they'd start a fight. Every time! Particularly at those old-fashioned two-day picnics—the first day was pretty well spoiled by them.

One day, Father Archie MacLellan was preaching his sermon on the Day of Judgment. He was quite a good preacher and he made a beautiful job of the sermon. He mentioned the fact that we'd all be together on the last day and, on the last day, everybody was going to be alive.

This old gentleman down back was doubting that this thing could happen at all. So, after Mass was over, he went into the glebe house and he said, "Father Archie, did you mean we were all going to be together on the Day of Judgment? We'd all be standing before the throne of God?"

"Oh yes," he said. "Yes, indeed, we will."

The old gentleman said, "Will Sandy and Alex be there?"

"Yes."

"Then there's one thing I want to tell you, Father. There'll be damn little judging done the first day!"

J1260. Repartee based on church or clergy

P251.5.3. Hostile brothers

153.

There was this one particular chap died in Inverness, and his nickname was Spotty. Poor Spotty died and his wife got somebody to make the casket. Lumber was scarce and Spotty was a big man and, when they made the casket, they used all the lumber and they squeezed poor Spotty in somehow.

Two of his neighbours came down, two old fellows. They went in and said their prayers and their respects. When they came out one fellow said to the other, "Well, poor Spotty is gone, isn't he?"

The other fellow said, "Yes and, Lord help us, didn't he look uncomfortable in there!"

J1440. Repartee—miscellaneous **V60. Funeral rites**

154.

They tell one about the fella that was so badly henpecked. His wife was continually after him. She was relentlessly scolding him or bossing him, and finally he was on his last illness. She used to be in the room with him all the time, ordering him, "Say your prayers, John. Take your medicine, John."

Finally, when she knew he was just about near the end, she took him by the hand and she started telling him what a beautiful life they'd lived together and he was wishing she would stop.

Finally she said, "John, you're going to go very soon and I won't be long after you."

With his last breath he said, "For God's sake, take your time!"

J1540. Retorts between husband and wife **T253. The nagging wife**

155.

This gentleman was a fixture at every wake and every wedding. Particularly the wakes, because he'd stay all night and there'd usually be tea made three or four times.

This particular day, he heard that one of his neighbours had died and the widow was left with three sons. Instead of putting a suit on the remains, they figured it was a waste, she decided to make a shroud from some brown cloth and hook it on the remains.

The lady was in a great hurry to get it made and she told her eldest son to go to Inverness, get the material and two boxes of icing sugar. She was going to make some cakes, do some baking for the night.

He wasn't coming home, so she sent the second fellow and, finally, she had to send the third son.

In the meantime, this gentleman who always attended the wakes was sitting in the house waiting for tea or something to happen.

Finally the first son came and he put two boxes of icing sugar on the table but said that he had forgotten the material for the shroud.

The same thing happened to the second fellow. And the third son came in and he put the two boxes of icing sugar on the table and he said, "Mama, the other boys must have gotten the material for the shroud so I didn't get it."

She threw up her hands and said, "In the name of the Lord, what am I going to do?"

The gentleman waiting for the tea was getting pretty angry and he said, "I'd suggest that you frost him!"

J1440. Repartee—miscellaneous

V60. Funeral rites

156.

This man was about eighty-five when he told me about a story he'd been told years earlier. It was about a young fellow who was unemployed and had hunted every place for work. He was almost in despair.

While he was walking along this road, he met a stranger. The stranger asked where he was going and he told him, "I'm looking for work and I don't care where I'll find it."

The stranger said to him, "Well, possibly I can fix you up. I'm going to do some work, not far from here, and I'll let you know before Monday. But, before I hire anybody, we sign a contract."

And he took a paper out of his pocket and he took a rather peculiar looking pen out of his pocket. He started to make his signature and he said, "My pen is empty. There's no ink. Just hold your hand out."

And gave the young man's hand a quick punch with the pen and drew a drop of blood.

"There, you can sign with the blood."

The stranger started to leave and the man noticed that he had a cloven hoof which indicated nothing else but the devil. Then the stranger disappeared.

The young man was in a pretty desperate condition and he remembered there were two very religious old ladies living in the neighbourhood. He went to them and he told them what had happened.

One of them said to him, "As good as we are to pray and all of that, we can't do very much for you, but we will try."

They took him out and they put him on a little hill above the house. They gave him a rooster and told him to hold it under his left arm, and they put a Bible on his head.

They said, "The devil is gonna come back. We don't know in what shape or when, but he's going to appear." And they began to pray over him.

In a very short time they saw a huge raven coming down. The Bible was opened, on his head, and the raven plucked a page out of the Bible and flew away with it. It came back and plucked another one.

The women told him, "If the rooster crows before the last page is torn from the Bible, you'll be saved."

According to the story, they were down to the second last page when the rooster crowed. Of course, the raven disappeared.

G303.3.3.3.2. Devil in form of crow

G303.4.5.3.1. Devil detected by his hooves

G303.17.1.1. Devil disappears when cock crows

K218.2. Devil cheated of his victim by boy having a bible under his arm

M201.1.2. Pact with the devil signed in blood

M211. Man sells soul to devil

157.

They tell some great stories about when the telephone was first introduced into this part of the country. Nobody knew anything about it and it was the greatest mystery in the world.

Many of the old people refused to believe that it was possible to speak over any instrument like that.

I heard a story about a couple from my own area. They had one daughter, away in the States. The old man refused to have anything to do with the telephone. He told his wife that it was nothing but an instrument of the devil.

Finally, his daughter came home from Boston and she persuaded them to put the telephone in the house. She tried to explain how good it would be, especially in the winter if anybody got sick. So, just to please her, the old man gave his consent, but still didn't think it was going to be of very much value. Then the daughter said she didn't want them to use the telephone till she went back to Boston. "The first phone call you'll receive will be from me."

One night, after the daughter had left, they were sitting in the kitchen and the phone rang. The old man went over to it, took it down, and he says, "Hello. Yes, I know." And he slammed the receiver down.

His wife said, "Was that Mary?"

"No," he said. "It was some damned fool saying, 'Long distance from Boston.' I learned that when I was in Grade Five!"

J2450. Literal fool

158.

A man in Inverness County—he was very satisfied with his home even though the toilet was out between the house and the barn. His two boys were away and they came home for a visit. Some friends were with them and they were a little bit embarrassed about the outdoor toilet and no bathroom in the house.

They finally decided they wanted to put a bathroom inside while they were home. The father agreed to it but the grandfather didn't want an indoor bathroom under any conditions.

So, the two boys discussed how they could get rid of that little outhouse. One of them said, "We're gonna get a stick of dynamite and we'll hook a long fuse to it. We'll get out behind the barn and we'll light the fuse. That toilet is going to go sky-high and that's all there'll be to it."

Unfortunately, while they were behind the barn lighting the fuse, they didn't notice that the grandfather had gone in for his morning comforts. He just got nicely settled with the catalogue when the whole thing went sky-high! Blew to pieces. It left the grandfather about half nude and kind of dazed. The boys came running from behind the barn, afraid they'd killed the old man, and he slowly got up and brushed himself off. He looked at the grandsons and he said, "Thank You, dear Lord, that I didn't let that one go in the house!"

J1810. Physical phenomena misunderstood

159.

This happened in the Margarees. A couple was expecting a baby and they were in complete poverty. No comforts of any kind.

Finally the night came when the baby was due. The husband went for the midwife and then they made the necessary preparations for the delivery.

The only light in the house was a lantern and, when the time actually arrived, he held the lantern to help the midwife out and light the baby's way into the world.

A baby was born and he was quite enthused about it. Then the midwife said, "Just a minute Sandy. There's another one on the way."

Sure enough, the second one was born and Sandy was a little disappointed. Then the midwife said, "Wait, wait. There's another one on the way."

Sandy said, "Yes, yes. I'm going to put out this lantern. It's the light that's drawing them!"

J1810. Physical phenomena misunderstood **T586. Multiple births**

160.

This particular wake was taking place, quite near the cemetery, in the Margaree area. Sandy, who delighted in attending all the wakes, went to Inverness on the mail truck. He got a couple of bottles and, when he came back, he decided that he'd take a shortcut to the wake, through the graveyard. He fell in the open grave and either knocked himself out or just decided it was comfortable enough there, and went to sleep.

He woke up about five o'clock in the morning. He said, "I woke up and the birds were twittering in the trees and the sun was up. I looked around and all I could see was headstones and I said to myself, If this is the Day of Judgment, I'm the first man up!"

J2311. Person made to believe that he is dead

161.

This happened when my uncle, Doctor Chisholm, was a Liberal Member. Federal Member. Those were the days when they had the nominations. The big debate was on and they'd be tearing into each other and all of this. Each person would have their own crowd. The Tories'd be in one place and the Liberals would be in another, and they'd be cheering for their man.

This one particular fellow was hollering, "Three cheers for Doctor Chisholm." And he'd keep on hollering this.

There happened to be a Conservative standing alongside of him, an old fellow, and he turned to him and said, "Oh, three cheers for the devil!"

The other fellow looked at him and he says, "Go ahead. You cheer for your man and I'll cheer for mine."

J1250. Clever verbal retorts—general

162.

Mose was down in Sydney, and some of the company he travelled around with was quite questionable. He had a very close relative in Sydney, a very, very respectable lady, and she just dreaded seeing Mose when he was on one of his binges. She loved to see him come to the house sober but she never knew what to expect.

She was going to a bridge party one afternoon. She and two of her lady friends were all dressed up and they were walking down one of the main streets. Who did they see coming up, pretty well loaded, but Mose, and he was latched onto the arm of a girl of quite questionable character.

She didn't want to say anything to him but she wanted him to know that she was noticing that he wasn't behaving himself properly. She says, "Good afternoon, Mose. I see you have acquired a new girl."

He turned to her right quick and he says, "Not new—slightly used."

J1300. Officiousness or foolish questions rebuked

J1321. The unrepentant drunkard

X520. Jokes concerning prostitutes **X700. Humour concerning sex**

163.

These two Sisters—they had a convent rather near the place where the Reverend Ian Paisley was staying. There was a group of Sisters there and the two went out one day on a journey. They had an old car and they visited many places. One of the things they'd be doing was a little charity work, helping old people and looking after them.

On their way back through one of these country districts in Ireland, they ran out of gas. They were stuck for a while until a fellow came along with a great big lorry. He stopped to see if they were in trouble and they told him they were out of gas. He said, "I could give you some gas but I have no container."

They looked all around and all they could find in the car was a chamber pot that they had been carrying around to, when necessary, relieve some of the old people they were visiting. They said, "Would this do?"

He said, "Yes, you can put the gas in it all right, but I'm in an awful hurry. I'll siphon the gas for you and you'll have to pour it in yourselves."

When he left, the two Sisters took the pot, and they were just beginning to pour it in the car when who comes along but the Reverend Ian Paisley. He stopped and he looked at them and watched for a bit. Then he said, "Sisters, I don't belong to your religion at all, but I admire your faith a great deal."

J1260. Repartee based on church or clergy

J1810. Physical phenomena misunderstood

PADDY MACDONALD

INVERSIDE

164.

Back in Scottish history, a lot of people believed in witches and curses and things like that. A lot of people had the belief that, if a person wanted to be in another place bad enough, they could wish themselves there.

This guy had moved to our area, from Scotland. He settled there and he was a single man.

Now, everybody used to go down to the shore to pick the cranberries, in the fall. Near the shore, there was a farm there and there was two barrens on it. There was the main barren and there was an outer barren for keeping hay on, and it was up near the cranberry barrens. So, as he was close to the bank of the ocean, he happened to glance down towards the beach.

There was three cats come out of the water. They come up the bank, passed through the cranberry barren and into a barn. Then he heard a noise and he glanced back—and there was three women emerged from the barn. Well, he was kind of stunned, you know, because he recognized them as three he had known in Scotland.

There was something had happened in Scotland that he knew of and they knew he knew. They recognized him and they made for him and they pounded the living hell out of him. They told him that if he was ever to mention their names, or who they were and where they came from, that the next time they would come back and they'd kill him.

He said that those people settled down in this area. I could name the places they settled but I don't want to. They raised families and they lived very good lives.

D644. Transformation to travel fast

G211.1.7. Witch in form of cat

G269.10. Witch punishes person who incurs her ill will

165.

There was a family, they were quite poor, and it was around Christmas time. They had a child and they were just making ends meet and they couldn't afford to buy anything as gifts. They would ask him, "Well now, Johnny, what would you like for Christmas this year?"

She'd be pregnant again, eh. "Would you like a little baby brother or a baby sister?"

He would say "yes," so, sure enough, at Christmas time there'd be a baby born.

This went on and the family was getting fairly big and he went to school. Got talking amongst some of the boys, a little bit older.

So, this year, the mother said to him, "Well, Johnny, what would you like to have for Christmas this year? Would it be a little baby boy or a baby sister?"

He says, "Well, Mom, if it wouldn't put you out of shape too much, I'd like to have a bike!"

J1930. Absurd disregard of natural laws **T570. Pregnancy**

166.

There were three ladies, they met. They were getting up in years so their discussion that day was age. One says, "Well, my God, it's awful to be getting old. A person gets so forgetful. When I would be walking down the street and I stop to talk to anyone I meet, I can't remember then if I was going one way or going the other way."

"Ah," the other one says, "isn't that it! Sometimes when I'll be going up the stairs, if I stop to catch my breath, then I can't remember if I was going upstairs or coming downstairs."

The third one, she didn't want to admit that she was getting in bad shape. So, she rapped on the table and, "Knock on wood," she says. "I'm as lucky as can be. My memory is as good as the day I was ten years old, and my heart and my lungs and my eyesight and my hearing. By the way, did any of you people hear someone rapping at the door?"

J2671. The forgetful fool

167.

Back some years ago, most of the people around here went to the lumber woods in the winter. A lot of them went to work in the lumber woods when they'd be going on to college. As it happened, Archie Neil here happened to be one of them.

Willy D. was working over in St. Ann's, so Archie was in need of some work, helping out before he'd go back to his following term. He spoke to Willy D. and Willy D. says, "Well, I'll see what I can do." Anyway, he told Archie Neil to go over and he would see the boss over there.

They decided that they would have a little fun, but Willy D. was after telling Archie Neil what to expect, when the boss would ask him if he had experience.

He asked Archie, "Have you any experience in the woods?"

"Oh, yes."

So, he showed him the mill. "What's that?'

"Well, that's a sawmill."

And the old crosscut. "What's that?"

"That's a crosscut."

"Well, we'll go in the woods and see how you are on the trees. What kind of a tree is that?"

Archie says, "That's a red spruce."

"Right you are. What's this one over here?"

"Well, that's a black spruce."

"Well, I see you're more experienced that I thought. Archie, we'll take a walk up the mountain a little farther."

Got up to where the trees were taller, forty feet without a limb, eh. "Now Archie, tell me, where's the front of this tree?"

Archie looked at it and he went and he walked around the tree. He said, "The front of it's right here."

The boss stopped for a second. He says, "How do you know that?"

"Well, there's somebody made his business behind this one."

H509. Tests of cleverness or ability: miscellaneous

J30. Wisdom (knowledge) acquired from inference

J1661. Clever deductions

168.

As far as ghosts are concerned, I'm not the bravest man in the world, but when I was younger I always pretended that I didn't believe in them.

So, we used to go off to dances, two and three of us, sometimes go to Port Hood. I used to hear an awful lot of ghost stories about in around Glencoe and Glencoe Mills.

We all went to this dance one night, in Harbourville, and I spotted this one that was sitting alone. She'd be mid-twenties, so I went and asked her to dance. Well, I had to make the quick rush and I asked if I could take her home, in the first set I danced with her, and she said okay.

As we started driving into Glencoe, there were a lot of vacant houses and everything seemed spookier and spookier. She said, "You're the first man I've been out with since my husband died."

"Oh," I said. It didn't dawn on me that she might have been married at one time, she looked so young.

Anyway, she said, "He died about three years ago."

I said, "Was it an accident?"

She said, "Yes, but he lived for a short time after."

"Good enough." I figured she would think that I was kind of timid.

So I went in, sitting in the parlour on a chesterfield. A big window behind, open. She went to the kitchen to make the tea. I took a book that was on the corner of the chesterfield and started reading it.

She was after describing what her husband looked like, on the trip home. So the door opened from the hall and I thought it was her coming through with the tea. I looked and—Lord God in heaven, here this guy was standing there. Just a dead image of what she'd described her husband to look like.

Well, boy oh boy, I just couldn't think of anything but I threw the book at him and the book just went clear through him, like if it went through a shadow. Then he started walking toward me.

I didn't waste any time. I just up and over the back of the chesterfield and out through the open window. And as I did, didn't he get hold of my ankle! He started pullin' my leg and pullin' my leg—same as I'm pullin' your leg now!

E221.3. Dead husband returns to reprove wife's second husband (lover)

Z13.4.1*. The storyteller escapes from a dangerous situation

169.

Some time ago a Cape Bretoner met up with a Scotsman and an Irishman, overseas somewhere. They decided to travel to some of the other countries and they landed in one of the Arab countries. Then they went broke and what'd they do but they robbed a little canteen or something. Just enough money to keep them going for a while, but they were caught by the police.

One law that they had was anyone caught stealing was put before the firing squad. The first fellow they took out was the Scotsman and he was wondering how in the name of God was he gonna get out of this.

When the commander said, "Ready, aim...," the Scotsman hollered, "Hurricane!" And they all took for shelter and away went the Scotsman.

They figured, well, they still had the Irishman and the Cape Bretoner left, and they took the Irishman out.

He thought, "By God, that worked for the Scotsman. I gotta come up with something."

So, when the commander hollered, "Ready, aim...," the Irishman hollered, "Earthquake!" Away they go again for shelter and the Irishman took off.

The Cape Bretoner was still in the pen and they came after him. He had noticed what the other fellas had done and he was thinking.

The commander said, "Ready, aim...," and the Cape Bretoner hollered, "FIRE!"

J2130. Foolish disregard of personal danger

X600. Humour concerning races and nations

170.

Now, you all know Fr. Stanley MacDonald, our parish priest at home. He was a man who didn't believe, at all, in ghosts or anything like that.

When he came to Inverness and Broad Cove, he stayed for a time at Inverness. Being fond of the country and the glebe house in Broad Cove was in fairly good shape, he decided that he would move out there. So, he got the people to get it livable and he moved out.

At this time he didn't have a housekeeper and there was no priest there to assist him so he found the place quite lonely. He'd heard quite a few stories about the glebe house in Broad Cove which he didn't pay much attention to.

During this particular night he woke up and he started getting this uneasy feeling. He just couldn't get back to sleep. He turned around in bed and thought he made out the form of a person standing at the foot of the bed. So he turned on the light and, sure enough, there was a person at the foot of the bed and he was a priest. He said to him, "I don't recognize you but I know that you are a clergyman."

The figure spoke to him and said, "Yes, I am. I was to come here some years ago but I never arrived. You're just starting out in this parish and there's three things I want you to do. The first one is, there's too much drinking going on in the parish. This is in all age groups. Now, I want you to try and do something about this.

"Secondly, the neighbours here are getting more apart, more distant, and they're becoming strangers within their own group. I want you to try and bring back the unity that they once had.

"The third thing, I'm not going to tell you now. If you accomplish those first two I'll return again."

Father Stanley promised that he would.

This priest had given his name and he was supposed to have been from Montreal. He was coming by boat and the boat sunk and he was drowned and he never arrived.

So, that's how he left Father Stanley, and Father Stanley expects to see him again.

There's a little comedy connected with the story. Father Stanley did start off immediately on his campaign to decrease the amount of drinking.

There was a chap around home who drank quite a bit and was quick with an answer. Father Stanley happened to be going by the Legion one day and this man was going in. He thought, "Well, here's my chance to start." He followed him in.

The guy was at the bar and he got a double whiskey. Father Stanley came in next to him and he says, "Just hold on a minute now. I'm gonna demonstrate something for you. Don't drink that till I come back."

Father Stanley went outside and when he came back in he had a worm. He dropped the worm in the whiskey. The worm died immediately and Father Stanley says, "Now, what do you think of that?"

The guy was thinking for a minute. Then he reached down and he picked the worm out of the whiskey, and he gulped it down. He says, "Well, all I can see, Father, is that if you drink plenty of whiskey you'll never have worms."

E338.1(fae). Ghost sits on foot of bed

E366. Return from dead to give counsel

E414. Drowned person cannot rest in grave

J1260. Repartee based on church or clergy

J1321. The unrepentant drunkard

ANNIE THE TAILOR MACPHEE

THE CORNER, INVERNESS

171.

These folks, they were older people, they used to invite a bunch of us young people down to play cards. The old lady was just a darling.

We were sitting down playing cards and she was making tea. Allan, the boy, said he was going out to the barn.

He went and, after awhile, the front door opened and this blast of wind came right through. Then it closed again.

We thought he came in through the front door because it was windy.

Then the front room window went up and we could hear, like, boards being fired in. You know?

We looked at one another, nobody seemed to pay attention. The old lady was making the tea, and we heard, every one of us that was playing the cards. But none of themselves heard it—the ones that were living in the house.

A couple of years after that, the old man died and we were there, one of the girls and I. We were helping the old lady make pies and things.

They were getting him ready. They were making the casket but they were going to put him on cold boards, as they called them. The boy said, "Well, there's boards out on the scaffolding in the barn. I'll go out and get them."

He went out to get the boards and when he came back, he took the lantern and he came into the porch and he tried to put the boards through. They wouldn't come through.

So, they put up the front room window and I remember perfectly well, while opening the oven door, I heard the front room window going up and these boards being put in. Fired in through the front room window.

I turned to this girl that was with me—she's dead today—and I said, "We heard that before."

She said, "I was just gonna say to you, we heard all that before."

And we did. We heard it years before it actually happened.

D1827.1.2.3*. Sound of coffin-making in carpenter shop before order for coffin is received

172.

I used to have a beautiful animal, a mare, with sleigh and everything.

Anyway, a friend of mine was walking the road one night and he saw this funeral coming to meet him.

He was only a young man.

He said the funny part of it was, the sleigh was ahead with the casket on it and right behind it was me. But there wasn't a sound out of my sleigh bells. There was no bells on the horse or anything.

I used to have so many of them things on the horse.

He said everything was quiet.

"And there was two women with you in the sleigh," he said. "And there was five or six more sleighs behind."

Well, the years went by and this old lady died. It was in January.

I went and, before I left home, my uncle filled up all the bells. You know, the shaft bells. Filled them up with wool or something. Closed them off. And no bells on the horse. I drove down there and I picked up the two daughters and took them.

Their mother had died and the casket was on the sleigh ahead and the rest were right behind me.

My friend just stood till everything went by and then he kept walking home.

D1825.7.1. Person sees phantom funeral procession some time before the actual procession takes place

173.

One time I went to stay with a girl friend, quite a piece from home. Her parents were gone away and they left the house all to ourselves.

Of course in them days there was no electric heat, just a wood stove. We had supper and we then talked around the wood stove for a while. Then we decided it was bedtime.

We lit the lamp and we took off for bed. Oh, the bed, it was cold but it was comfortable. Lots of clothes on it. We talked for a while, then we fell asleep.

By golly, I woke up and was frozen, and she said, "I'm freezing! What's wrong?"

"We got no clothes on," I said.

We looked and all the clothes were gone off the bed. So we got up, one on each side of the bed, and we hauled the clothes back on. We were only teenagers. We crawled in under the clothes, put them around our shoulders and settled down for the night.

After a while, the same thing happened over again. Two or three hours later we woke up and, again, were frozen and no bedclothes.

This time we started getting a wee bit shaky so we decided, well, we might as well pull the clothes on and, this time, stay awake. We dragged up the clothes, crawled in under them and tucked them in as well as we could, and we waited there.

Everything was quiet and she said, "We might as well put the light out now."

We put the light out and we settled down. After a while, the bedclothes start going, going and going, little by little, down towards the foot of the bed.

We started getting kind of scared then. We were pulling them back up and still there was something pulling them away from us. So, we decided there's a power stronger than us that's pulling the clothes off us. We got up and lit the lamp and pulled them back up again.

We settled for a while and stayed like we were going to go to sleep. But we didn't sleep and it went again. This time I hopped out of bed and I said, "This is enough of this. Let's go and build a fire in the wood stove and sit by it the rest of the night."

That's what we did.

E279.3. Ghost pulls bedclothing from sleeper

174.

I lived in a house there and I stayed there, overnight, all by myself. There was a bedroom off the kitchen and I decided I was going to sleep there for the night.

Through the night, the front door would open and I'd hear, like, workboots going upstairs. You know, climbing upstairs. There was rooms upstairs and the steps were going into separate rooms.

There was nobody to come near the place at night. The folks were away, they went on a trip.

So, the doors would slam shut. Somebody else would come and go upstairs.

Later on, about forty years after that, the house was used as a lumber camp. They were using the front door for the lumbermen to come in and, upstairs, they had their bunks.

And that's what I was hearing that night.

D1827. Magic hearing **E402.1.2. Footsteps of invisible ghost heard**
E402.1.7. Ghost slams door

Malcolm MacDonald

LOWER RIVER INHABITANTS AND DUNVEGAN

175.

This happened at Port Hood station. You notice how far Port Hood station was from the store? Travellers used to come, get their orders from Port Hood and rush for the hobo train coming down in the afternoon.

Anyway, one fellow just made it, you know. Kind of a fat traveller. When he got there he was panting, so he sat down.

First thing, he started grumbling, "I don't know why in the hell they put the station so far from the town."

And this fellow spoke up, "They wanted to have it handy the railroad."

J1252. Quibbling answers

176.

This politician died. He was a wonderful man and St. Peter wasn't long before he went over his record and everything.

He said, "You were a wonderful man down there on earth. You were good to your voters and good to everybody. Now, there's no reason why you can't get right in here. Go right in and you'll be well looked after. Keep right on, there's nothing to keep you back. After a while, we'll get you going for wings and all that."

All right, he went in.

When he got in, there was a big lineup to the table where they were fed. So, he kept going and he went right to the head of the line.

The fellow behind says, "Get back to the end of the line."

"No, no. I don't have to. I was down on earth there and I did such wonderful work, I was never slighted. I was always waited on ahead of anybody else."

"Everybody is equal here," they said. "Get back in the line."

Well, he went back of the line and him grumbling.

After a little while, a six-foot, good-looking man come in. Well dressed and humming a tune. He walked right up to the head of the line and here, they turned around and gave him his tray and put all his food on it.

He went over to a table and sat down.

This politician said, "Look. Look at this now. I thought everybody was equal here! Look what they did to that fella."

Fellow at the table says, "Hush, hush. That's Christ. He comes in here for breakfast every morning."

F11. Journey to heaven (upper-world, paradise)

J1260. Repartee based on church or clergy

177.

I never believed in the ouija board. In fact, I never saw one till here about in the early 'seventies, I think it was.

There was an election here and I had to drive this lady home. We had to go to her mother's place to pick up some of her little ones. On the way home we both said, "We'll drop into this house here. They have a television and we'll get the election reports."

So, we went up to this house and here was a married woman and a teenage girl, at the kitchen table, with the ouija board.

I looked and I said, "It's the first time I ever saw a ouija board."

"Well, do you want to ask it a question?" she said.

"What d'ya mean? The question in my mind or do I have to speak up?"

"Oh, I'd rather for you to speak up," she said.

"Well," I says, "okay. Ask the ouija board if I got a ten-dollar bill in my pocket?"

See, the "no" in one corner and the "yes" on another corner and then the row of numbers and everything else. Letters on the ouija board.

So anyway, the thing circled around. They were holding the tips of their fingers on it. When they asked if Malcolm had a ten-dollar bill in his pocket, it circled around and around and went up to the "no."

"Well, there it is. Have you got a ten-dollar bill?"

I says, "No. Ask the board if I got a five-dollar bill?"

It circled around again and their fingers followed it. Went up to "no" again.

"Have you got a five-dollar bill?"

I said, "No, I haven't."

There was twice it told the truth.

I said, "Ask the board if I got a fifty-dollar bill in my pocket?"

They went to work and they asked the board. Away the thing goes and went right up to "yes"—and they looked at me.

"Ask the board if I got another fifty-dollar bill?"

It went right up to "yes" again.

Anyway, to make a long story short, it went four times, up to the "yes," and they said, "Have you got four fifty-dollar bills?"

"Ask the board, how many fifty-dollar bills I have in my pocket?"

It swung around and it came to the figure "8."

"Have you got eight fifty-dollar bills?"

I said, "Count them for yourself."

There they were. And that's the first time I ever saw a ouija board.

D1810. Magic knowledge

178.

Evil eye. People used to believe in that.

Well, this particular time, I remember myself. I was young, my father was visited by a friend of his. A close friend.

My father used to do his best, or whatever he could, around sick animals and all this and that. So, this fellow come and he said, "I have a sick horse at home. Would you mind coming with me?"

My father said, "Okay."

He had, like they did in those days, a nice horse for the buggy, and he said, "This mare's standing back in the stall since ten or twelve days. Won't eat or drink."

Well, my father went with him.

The first thing they did was look in her mouth, to see if there was any teeth or anything bothering her. He examined the mare and not a thing could be found.

Still, she wouldn't eat or drink.

My father asked him, "Where was the last place you were with her?"

He said he was at a certain person's place. "I don't believe in it," he said, "but everybody told me that man had an evil eye."

"Well, what'll we do?" my father asked. "Should we put her in the buggy and go up and visit? I'd like to visit those people anyway."

"How can that mare, in that condition, pull the two of us and the buggy?"

"Well, we'll go late in the evening, when there's nobody travelling."

So, they hitched up and they walked along with the mare. They had to go about two miles or maybe a little better.

They went and they visited at this house, had a sociable visit. When they were leaving this old man came out with them. It was bright enough that he could see this little mare, that he was so used to and always looked so nice.

He says, "What's this in the shafts? What happened to the mare?"

"She never ate a bite or drank a drop of water, since I was here before."

"Well," he said, "I remember that. My God, that's tough. I'm sorry. I'm awfully sorry to see her that way."

Anyway, they went back, my father and the other fellow. Got back to the fellow's barn, stripped her off and put her in the stall.

She walked up to the manger and started to eat and drink.

She got well after that.

D2071. Evil eye

G265.4.2.2*. Witch causes illness of horse

179.

This old lady, she was hard up for a pair of shoes. She visited all the neighbourhood and there was one place in particular, a young couple with no family. They were very much in love with each other and got along so good. When she'd visit, if the man was away at work, the lady used to talk so well of the husband. What a lovely man he was and they were getting along so good.

When he'd be home he'd talk the same way about his wife.

Anyway, this one was desperate to get the pair of shoes. She'd been hinting in different places and at this particular place, but she wasn't getting the shoes. Hers were pretty well worn out and the cold weather coming.

She left that house for home, and she started wishing she'd see the devil. She was that desperate. After a little, a man appeared. She spoke, "Who are you?"

"I'm the devil," he said.

"What can I do for you?"

"Well, I guess you're desperate about getting a pair of shoes."

"Yes, I'd do anything to get a pair of shoes."

"Well listen," the devil said, "if you can help me, I think I can help you and get them shoes for you."

"What have I got to do?" she asked.

"You try and break up that couple that's getting along so good with each other. I tried every way to do it already and I failed. If you can help me, I'll get you the shoes."

She went back on the following day, went in and the lady was alone. The lady was nice to her and gave her a cup of tea and started talking about the husband again, how happy she was and how happy she lived.

The old lady said, "Isn't it too bad you haven't got a family?"

She said, "Yes, but we'll have to forget that part of it."

The old lady says, "I think I could help you."

"How could you help?"

"I'll just tell you. This evening, when your husband comes home, give him his supper and do everything the way you usually do and get him to go to bed early. Tell him you'll do the chores and he'll be willing to do that, I'm sure."

She said, "Yes, I'll do that."

"When he goes to sleep, you go upstairs, get his razor and shave some of the hair right below here, on his neck. Just shave a little of it off and I'm sure everything will be in order. You'll have a family after that."

When he come home from work she had supper all ready. She said, "Now, John, being's you're so tired, you go to bed and I'll finish my work. You go to bed and sleep and I'll be up after a while."

After he was sound asleep, the wife went up and she got the straight razor. She went in on her tiptoes and she pulled down the collar of his pajamas and she was going to cut those few little hairs off. He woke up and he saw the razor. He upped with a right and got her in the jaw! Knocked her cold on the floor, put the kicks to her and they broke up right there, that night.

The next night, the old lady was out and she met the devil. "Listen," says the devil, "I have the shoes but I can't pass them directly to you. I'll put them on the end of this cane—because you're far worse than I am!"

1353 The Old Woman as Troublemaker

D2161.3.11. Barrenness magically cured

K1085. Woman makes trouble between man and wife: the hair from his beard

M210. Bargain with the devil

PETER RANKIN

MABOU

180.

This picnic, or whatever it was, came off, and they were after cutting the hay with a hand scythe. I guess they could drive her then, with the hand scythe. And there was a couple of days they didn't show up, Archie and Ranald.

Archie came to the door and Father John came, I guess with no smile on, and said, "Well, well. Where were you?"

"I was with Ranald."

"I see. And where was Ranald?"

"Ranald was with me."

"I see. And where were the two of you?"

"We were together."

J1252. Quibbling answers

181.

During the Depression days, they used to ride on the bus to Port Hood Mines. I forget who was driving the bus, but Shorty Campbell was around and a few more and Rory coming with a bottle of what we called "black tea" in his hip pocket.

Well, I remember that puddle that used to be right at Archie Campbell's store. Rory was coming and the bus was waiting and one foot went away up in the air and down comes Rory, plunk. The bottle went to splinters.

Rory turned around, looked at the bottle and the frozen puddle. He says, "July will fix you, you son-of-a-bitch!"

J1891. Object foolishly blamed

KATIE ANN CAMERON

GLENCOE STATION

182.

Down Gillis's Meadow, there was one night that they went and I guess they were digging and digging and, I guess, they struck something, you know. But somebody spoke and, once you speak, that's it. It disappeared.

Then they went down another night and, whatever happened, they looked up in the sky. The moon was shining and there was a little black ball up on the moon.

They didn't pay no attention to it and it was spreading and spreading. Then the sky opened and it started. Hailstones.

They had a lantern and it broke the chimney on it and they were in the dark. Well, they had to quit.

Then, the crowd of them, they went to this house. They picked up a stone and they took the stone with them. When they were sick and tired of looking at this stone, they threw the stone in the chimney. This house had a fireplace, the chimney they used to call it.

I guess every cow and every bull and every bird and every thing that was in the world was coming down that chimney. They had to take the stone and throw it outside and still it was bothering them.

So, they told this person, "You have to take that stone back where you got it or you won't have any peace."

And that's what they had to do. They had to take the stone back to where they got it. Where they were digging for the money.

And there was no more.

D931. Magic rock (stone)

N550.1. Continual failure to find or unearth hidden treasure

N553.2. Unlucky encounter causes treasure-seekers to talk and thus lose treasure

N581. Treasure guarded by magic object

183.

I was looking out one day and I seen this group of people. I said to the ones in the house, "What's going on? What's going on?"

"Nothing. There's nothing out there but snowbanks."

"Well," I said, "there's something going on. There's a whole group of men goin' over the field."

"We don't see nothing."

"Well, I see them," I said. "There's six or seven of them there."

"Och, you're crazy."

"No, I'm not," I said.

About ten years after that, they were putting the power line through our place and these were the six.

"Now," I says, "who'll tell me I'm crazy?"

That's true. I seen it before it happened.

D1825.7.1. Person sees phantom funeral procession some time before the actual procession takes place

Sid Timmons

NEW WATERFORD AND MARGAREE CENTRE

184.

I made a song about the bosses. Went up to work one morning and my lamp was stopped. So I asked them what my lamp was stopped for. "See the manager."

I went up to the offices. "What's my lamp stopped for?"

"Go home," he said. Wouldn't even talk to me.

Next morning I went up. He says, "I told ya to go home."

I wanted some reason so I went up in the afternoon. He got up and closed the door. "Sit down. Now, my friend, the next time you have poetical illusions, you carry them out in your own home!"

H503.1. Song duel **P415. Collier**

185.

If a horse broke his leg, they generally killed him right there in the mine, with a maul—if they were sure the leg was broke. If not, they'd load him on what they call a tram. It was the bottom of a box with no sides. Just flat. He was sent to the surface and, if he couldn't walk, they'd take him right into the stable and unload him in the box stall.

Sometimes the doctor'd come over and look at him and, if it was a serious injury, they'd destroy the horse right there, and burn him.

If it was an injury they thought they could cure, the ambulance came. It was a double team of horses and it had a divider in it so two horses could stand up. That was removable, if the horse couldn't stand; and they could winch him right into the wagon and take him to the hospital at Sterling Yard, in Glace Bay.

The stalls there were all made with four-by-four, instead of partitions, so a horse couldn't jam you. You could step between them into the next stall. There was a chart behind each horse: what mine he was from, his age, his colour and his name.

They took his temperature. Dr. MacIsaac's wife, the day I was there, that's what she was doing. She'd come along and stick the thermometer in their rectums, turn and talk to some fellows, pull it out and say, "Oh, he's a lot better today."

Then they had a kind of surgery. All the bottles of disinfectant and everything was there and, across from it, there was a sunken part of the floor. Some of the horses' feet would get real hard so they'd fill that with creoline solution, back the horses down into it and soak their feet in the solution.

The operating table was three pieces and hinged. You could turn the horse off its feet. You could spread his legs. Whatever position you wanted to put him in.

Everything was snow white, disinfected, just like in a regular hospital.

B802. Horses in tales and legends
F950. Marvelous cures **P415. Collier**

186.

One side of Heelan Street, in Waterford, wasn't built up. It was a coal company pasture. Was well fenced and, when the strike came in 1925, they took the horses out of Number 12 mine, brought them around the road and put them in this field. Each morning they were checked by the stable man and a company policeman.

There was one old mare there, she'd been in the pit a long, long while. She had no eyes. Her eyes were out. There was a violent thunder storm this night and, in the morning, there was one horse missing and she was the one. They couldn't locate her anywhere until they found her in her own stall approximately a mile from the surface.

That was the only home she knew. Her blind, and she found her way.

P415. Collier **U130. The power of habit** **X1241.2. Well-trained horse**

187.

My horse was hurt one time. There was a Marsh boy there and he had a wonderful black horse by the name of Toby.

I come out and there was six boxes there, and my brother said to Marsh, "Give Sid your horse. He's gonna take them six boxes so he'll catch up."

While I was in they decided, out handy on the landing, to shoot the place. They fired a shot and the place caught fire. I was the only driver inside and the owner of the horse come in and he said, "She's a-fire outside. Run to the low level and tell the men."

I said, "You go to the low level, I'll go to the counter level."

I hooked the horse off and I said, "Go, Toby." He looked at me, like that, and I said, "All right, stay there b'y."

I thought I could run but I couldn't run alongside some of those old fellows! They were passing me like I was tied.

When I come out I told my brother, "My horse is inside." He was talking to the superintendent and they were all excited. They called for volunteers to gather up some of the horses.

I remember, we had eleven horses going up to the stable. That evening, seven o'clock, they got to the level and here was my horse, Toby. He was down on his knees, his head down handy the rails to keep clear of the smoke.

P415. Collier

X1241.2. Well-trained horse

188.

They claim the company got forty dollars for a man and fifty dollars for a horse—insurance. I don't know if that was true or not but that's what they claim.

See, if you were breaking in horses they'd say to you, "If ya can't work him, kill him." Because they couldn't get fifty dollars for a bad horse when you'd come up. The word'd get around the horse was no good and nobody'd buy him. Generally sold for twenty-five dollars or so.

B802. Horses in tales and legends

P415. Collier

189.

There was one big red mare, a beauty, and Johnny MacNeil took her out the first day. Well, as a rule, you'd run an empty box in and out and maybe a full one that day. She seemed to catch on to her work pretty well so Johnny hauled two out, two or three times.

The word went up—the new mare worked great—and they took her out again that night. They started hauling six ton at a time with her. They worked her that night, they worked her the next day, the next night and, the fourth day, she quit. She would not move regardless of what you did.

I was breaking in horses just then. The underground manager, Livingston—he was killed in West Virginia—come along and he says, "How about taking her out and trying her."

I harnessed her up, spoke to her. She wouldn't move. No, boy. So I pushed the box and she'd walk ahead of it, when I'd push it.

I hooked her off and let her walk in with the shafts on. Walked out, do anything, go anywhere with the shafts. Swung her around and hooked on again and—no.

Well, I had a whip, six plaits of leather, rawhide, and the handle was a piece of a cue stick loaded with lead. I got the box and I give her a couple of touches. When she took off, she was wide open and I knew she'd kill me the speed she was travelling. I leaned out and pulled on the reins and she stopped stone dead and fell down. I knew she'd struck her head. Of course, there was a heavy cap on the bridle, you know, double padding. But she couldn't get up.

I only felt sorry for two that I killed but, anyhow, we got her loaded and we took her to the stable and rolled her off. She was ice cold. I covered her up with hay and put bags over her. The stable man come along and said, "Sid, how about watering some horses?"

I was watering the third horse and he hollered, "The mare is dead!"

Her skull was cracked, she hit that hard. We checked it with a road nail.

She'd have killed me at the speed she was going, and she'd have been in China that evening.

B802. Horses in tales and legends

P415. Collier

190.

There was quite an attachment for a boy and his horse in the mine. You know? A lot of them became attached to their horse very much. Some of them, if their horse got killed, they'd cry just like it was their mother. Yeah, some of them never went back. They wouldn't go back driving any more if they lost their horse.

B802. Horses in tales and legends

P415. Collier

Joe Delaney

ST. JOSEPH DU MOINE

191.

This is supposed to have happened at Southwest Margaree but I don't want to say for sure.

This bachelor, he was going on sixty years of age and he hadn't made his Easter duties. So there we were at the Saturday before the Holy Trinity and he comes in the house after supper. Mother said, "Didja go to confession?"

"No."

"Well, you're gonna go right now."

So, he went. When he got there, the priest was all through hearing confessions so he went in by the kitchen door of the glebe house.

There was a bazaar or a picnic coming up shortly after the Holy Trinity and this guy didn't have any shoes. He only had enough money to go to the bazaar or the picnic.

Going down the hallway, he noticed a pair of shoes up against the wall. He takes the shoes and he puts them outside the front porch and he closed the door.

Then he knocked at the priest's office door and he told the priest, "Father, I want to make my Easter duties and I only got till tomorrow. I wanna go to confession."

"Come right in."

He knelt down and confessed all his sins. Got through with what he thought he had and says, "Father, there's another one."

"What is it?"

"Father, I confess having stolen a pair of shoes."

The priest said, "You're gonna have to return them to the owner."

"Well, will you take them, Father?"

"No, I don't want them. You're gonna have to return 'em to the owner."

"Well, Father, I offered him the shoes and he doesn't want to take them."

"Well keep them! They're yours!"

K373. "Owner has refused to accept it"

BUDDY MACMASTER

JUDIQUE

192.

This is a little story that I heard my uncle tell, and he's not a man that would tell lies or make up stories. This would be in the 'Thirties.

My uncle had an automobile, and there was a death in the community, so they decided to go to the wake. When they arrived at the wake house, the women went in immediately and they stood out in the yard. It was quite dark and they were talking. I think they had a little flask but they were sober. You know, they did have a little under their belt.

They were talking there and one fellow said to the other, "Are you seeing anything?"

"Yes, I am and I was wondering if I was imagining things. Are you seeing that too?"

He said, "Yes."

Apparently, there was a brightness from about the roof of the barn down to the ground, on a slant. So, they looked and here this well-dressed man, in black suit and hat, walked down from this brightness. Like it was a walkway, you know, and disappeared in the darkness.

After a while, the man came back out of the darkness and back up the bright walkway and disappeared in the darkness above the barn. Apparently, he did this a couple of times.

The third time, John MacIsaac said, "I'm gonna ask that fella who he is and what is he doing here?"

Sure enough, the fellow came back again and John said, "Who are you and what the hell are ya doing around here?"

The fellow didn't say anything. He walked out of sight.

After a while, back comes a big, black dog.

And that was the end of the vision. They thought maybe it was the devil that was around. I've asked both men, since then, if that was true and they said yes.

E752.2. Soul carried off by demon (Devil)

G303.3.1.2. The devil as a well-dressed gentleman

G303.3.3.1.1(a). Devil in form of black dog

G303.6.3.4. Devil appears in an intense light and with strong odor of sulphur

DONALD MACKAY

CHIMNEY CORNER

193.

There was an old lady lived—I don't remember her but I heard so much about her—Mary Bheag MacKay. She was a recluse. She used to keep cattle, which she didn't have enough hay to feed. Apparently, in the wintertime, she would come down to the shore, from the rear of Chimney Corner, perhaps down this way too to the Forks, and she'd get a bundle of hay from somebody and she'd carry it on her back. Get enough to pull her cattle through the winter.

She died at our old house, somewhere around 1912.

My son, he was brought up mainly in Newfoundland. He never lived here but when I come over here in 1972, he come over to spend a year with me in '73. He went to school here, at the Forks. He was about sixteen.

This was in November '73, and he got himself a small game license. He went hunting partridge, and darkness came on and he didn't show up. I got a little concerned. However, at just about dark, he come out of the woods right at our old place. I said, "Didja get lost?"

He said, "Yes, I did. I got bewildered and I sat down on a fallen tree. Then, I saw this old lady coming toward me with a long, black dress and carrying a bundle of hay on her back."

Right away, my ears picked up because, as soon as he mentioned the hay, I thought of Mary Bheag.

He said, "She come up to where I was and I asked her how do I get out to MacKay's. She never answered me. She just turned around and pointed—and she just disappeared, like that."

He said, "I went in the direction that she pointed."

And that's where he come out, right at our old house.

Now, I have no reason to believe that he could have known anything about Mary Bheag.

Last winter I went to Germany—he's serving in the armed forces over there—and we were sitting around talking in the evening. I said, "Tell me what happened to you when you were over with me in 1973. Do you remember that old lady? Could you draw her?"

He sat down and he drew a picture of her.

Now, I would have no idea what she looked like but, about a month after I got home, I was talking to an old gentleman and I asked him if he remembered Mary Bheag.

And he said, "Oh yes, quite well. I was at her funeral. I often saw her."

So I pulled this out of my pocket and I passed it to him. "Is that her?"

He looked very shocked. He said, "That is her! Who drew that?"

I said, "My son drew it—Danny."

He said, "That is her. That is Mary Bheag."

E363.2(e). Ghost warns person of approaching death

F571.3. Very old woman

Donald A. MacLellan

SOUTHWEST MARGAREE

194.

When I went to Boston, I got to know some people there. I got to know this young fellow, about my own age. He was an American, born up there. So, he and I used to go out now and again.

This night, we were meandering around, didn't know just exactly what to do, when we saw two girls coming down the street. He points to me and he said, "Listen, you leave these girls with me. I'm the boy that's gonna make the dates with those girls."

You see, I was from Cape Breton and a little dumb.

Up he comes to the girls and he started the gab and the talk and I was listening. He finally broached onto a date. Well, they were a little reluctant to make a date with us but, finally, they looked at each other and one said, "Okay, boys. We'll go out with ya Saturday night."

Oh, my friend just shivered with the thrill of thinking that he was going to go out with a girl.

"And how will we get in touch with you?" the fellow said.

One of the girls said, "I'll give you a telephone number here. You call this number at 7:30 Saturday night and, when you get an answer, ask for Kitten."

Well, I smiled to myself. We're going to go out Saturday night with two kittens.

We went home and Saturday night couldn't come fast enough. Finally Saturday did come and my friend called me up and he says to me, "You come over to my room. It's from my room we'll call them and I'll do the calling."

The poor Cape Bretoner went over there and we were sitting around till finally, 7:30 came. He used the telephone, he rung up, there was no answer the first time. The second time, an answer came, "Boston Cat Hospital!"

Well, he lowered his head and I turned to him and I said, "Why don't you ask for Kitten?"

Then I made a big, Cape Breton laugh and I told him, "Perhaps it's better to be a little dumb than to be too smart."

J2346. Fool's errand

K1218. Importunate lovers led astray

Angus MacDonald

GLENDALE

195.

I had an uncle, by marriage, who told a story about one time when a young man, he worked for this farmer down in the lower end of Dunvegan. It came on fall and there was some grain he wanted taken to the mill. Apparently the mill was somewhere up around Scotsville.

So, he went with the horse and cart and got there late in the afternoon. They started the threshing and, come dark, they were still at it. So the man that owned the mill decided they'd close down for the night and that he could stay.

When it was time to go to bed the mill owner gave him a lamp and showed him the room, up in the loft. It was a beautiful, clear night.

He got on his knees, said his prayers and got into bed. He happened to turn to the wall when, suddenly, someone jumped in behind him!

He took to praying. He didn't have the heart to turn around, he was so scared. He knew he didn't see anyone come in the door or in the window. He claimed he prayed all night.

Whoever was in the bed with him kept on turning one way, turn the other, and he thought many times to ask, "Who are you?"

So, at the break of day he thought, "I'll make sure that I'll see him before he leaves." But at the light of day, whoever it was disappeared.

Shortly afterwards, he heard the lady of the house down in the kitchen, so he got up. The husband and wife was there and she was holding a baby in her arms and she was making the porridge. They asked, "How did you sleep last night?"

He said, "Who in the hell was sleeping with me last night?"

The man looked at his wife, she looked at him—and there was no more said. They had their breakfast, then went out and started the mill. They got the rest of the grain threshed and he started off for home.

When he did get back he was telling the story to the man he worked for. He said, "Yes, I've heard that one of their sons was killed. In the wintertime, he went out to cut the ice around the wheel that provided the water power. As he was cutting the ice, the wheel got hold of him and dragged him under."

Apparently, this was the room that the man slept in and other people had slept there and had the same experience. He claimed that, never afterwards, was he scared. Perhaps from the praying all night long.

I heard him tell the story many, many times—and it never changed.

E324. Dead child's friendly return to parents

E472. Revenant sleeps in same bed with living but without contact

196.

A few years ago, I was sitting in this room and Father Rankin was having a shave. At that time he had a big Scotch dog and there was a knock came at the door. It was around one in the afternoon. Father said, "Go and see who it is."

I looked out, and the dog was still lying back in the hallway, and there was no one there. I came back and I said, "Father, there's no one there."

He said, "Well, someone'll be there tomorrow."

The following day, sure enough, a man came to the door. Someone had died over in the direction of West Bay Road.

D1827.1.3.1*. Rapping heard as death warning to hearer or friend of hearer

E402.1.5. Invisible ghost makes rapping or knocking noise

197.

An uncle was telling me about one of his experiences in Maine, working in the lumber woods. They had a boss who was used to going on a little spree for about two weeks. This time he went away and stayed longer than usual.

The bunkhouse and the cookhouse were attached and, this night, they heard an awful noise. It was like someone was breaking up the dishes in the cookhouse. Pots and pans coming down.

There were about thirty people in the bunkhouse and no one would get up to see what was wrong. One man had a revolver and he started firing through the wall into the cookhouse. Still, the noise kept on for an hour or so.

In the morning, when they got up, someone went into the cookhouse, and the only dishes that were broke were the ones that were done by the shots from the revolver.

Later, one of the drivers came into the camp and told them that their boss had died and they had to get something to put his body in. They took the box that all the dishes were in down from the wall, and got the man's body and took him back to the camp to be buried.

Possibly a forerunner.

D1827.1 Magic hearing of noises which portend death

E402.1.8. Miscellaneous sounds made by ghost of human being

HUGHIE J. CHISHOLM

GLENDALE

198.

I had an uncle, by the name of Colin, used to drive the stagecoach from Port Hastings to Whycocomagh. That was before the time of the railroad. He'd be going through into the head of the bay at Whycocomagh, late at night. As you know, there's a water pipe there but, at that time, there was a wooden trough where they used to water their horses. For many a night, he used to meet two little lights at this trough—and they'd follow him right into the village, then disappear.

There was a girl from Whycocomagh. She was going away to Boston and she took passage with Colin to Port Hastings this night. A very nice girl. She sang songs all the way.

She was only a week in Boston when she died, and he was the one who took her remains from Hastings to Whycocomagh. Right at this spot, where he used to see the lights, her father and mother met her. Two or three other teams went ahead of them—and those were the lights.

E530.1.7. Ghost light indicates route funeral will take

199.

This concerns two old maids that lived together. One of them, she would often become sure she was going to die and would send for the priest.

This particular night happened to be in the wintertime and there was quite a bit of a storm going on. The priest told the handyman, who stayed with him, to go out and get the horse ready and the sleigh.

The priest was used enough to going out there different times before and, every time he'd get there, there was nothing wrong with her. Anyway, since he got the call, he figured he'd better go, just in case.

So this guy got the horse and sleigh to the door and the priest went to the church and got the oils and everything and they headed out towards the place.

When they got to the door, the priest gave him a nudge. He says, "Look at her. Look at her in the window looking out at us! Nothing wrong with her."

The guy turned to the priest and said, "Father, you go in and anoint her and I'll be damned if I won't go in and knock her out!"

J1260. Repartee based on church or clergy

K1860. Deception by feigned death (sleep)

JIM MACKAY

WEST BAY ROAD

200.

Several years ago I used to travel for a tailoring firm, with tailoring samples, taking orders for suits and clothing. It took me to a lot of isolated spots, mostly in Inverness County.

I went on foot, of course, and I travelled mostly the side roads, down lanes and across the fields. I always spent the night in a different house, on that account. After walking all day, I'd be tired and very pleased to get a place for the night.

I remember this time, during October, when the nights can be pretty long and dark and dreary. I came to this farmhouse, and I'd known the people previously from visits during the day, but this time I arrived a bit late and they asked me to remain for the night.

We sat around for a while after supper. It was an old farmhouse, no electricity, so when it came bedtime they gave me a little lamp and showed me to a little room way down at the end of the hall.

It was only a very tiny room, just a shade bigger than would accommodate the bed. One window.

When I was ready for bed, I said my prayers. Afterwards, I was sorry I didn't say more.

I put out the light and it was then that it dawned on me how really dark it was. You could hardly discern the window. After a spell, I fell asleep.

I was wakened during the night by a terrific noise. You know, when you're awakened with a jolt you can't get your bearings in a hurry. It really shook the house and, to me, it sounded as if you dumped a cartload of stone against the outside wall. This frightened me, naturally, and I had no light, not even a match.

After a little, my bed was shaken just as if there was a giant on each corner of it. Vigorously. I said to myself, "This is the limit. He's really here now."

I felt, at first, that I would be able to skedaddle but it was pitch dark and I didn't know the house. I figured I'd bump into something if I got up. So, I decided as long as I didn't see anything I was content. I eventually went back to sleep and that was the end of it. I never mentioned it to the folks in the morning.

That was about all there was to it. I certainly got a deuce of a fright.

E338.1(f). Ghost haunts bedroom

201.

This story is from my father's father's time. There was a family by the name of Beck lived a couple of farms from us. One evening there was a man arrived at their house, on foot. He asked to be put up for the night.

There were still chores to do and they didn't pay too much attention. It appears that they never asked him his name or where he had come from or where his destination was. They did their chores, had supper, sat around a bit and then they showed him his room for the night.

When morning came, there was no sign of the man getting up. They had breakfast, did the morning chores, then sat down to think what might be keeping the man in bed. They wondered if he got up during the night or very early in the morning and kept going on his way. The woman of the house told the old man, "You better have a look to see if he's still there."

He went down to investigate and the man was dead in bed. They didn't know who he was or where to return him.

'Twas a mystery and a sad story.

H976. Task performed by mysterious stranger

J21.41.2. "A stranger does not close his eyes in sleep lest he close them in death"

N330. Accidental killing or death

John Duncan MacDonald

PORT HASTINGS

202.

A gentleman took off one morning, from Whycocomagh, going to Port Hastings. Around dinner time he was just approaching Glendale and he figured he'd get a good meal. So, he went to a house and was just in time. He sat down and had a big meal, had a smoke and rested for about an hour. Just when he was leaving, he asked the man of the house, "How far would it be to Port Hastings?"

"Seven miles."

So, he took off walking and landed in Queensville. He picked out a good house for a cup of tea, went in there, had tea. They were glad to see him. They talked back and forth for about half an hour and he figured he'd take off so he'd make Port Hastings before dark. Just when he was leaving, he turned to the man of the house and said, "How far would it be to Port Hastings?"

"Seven miles."

He didn't say a word and took off walking. He walked and he walked until he figured he walked about seven miles. He met a man coming with a horse and wagon. They talked some. Then he asked, "About how far would it be to Port Hastings?"

"Seven miles."

He said, "Thank God I'm not losing!"

J1442. A cynic's retorts **J1560. Practical retorts: hosts and guests**
X583. Jokes about travelers

ARCHIE A. MACNEIL

CREIGNISH

203.

Hector Doink was working in the lumber woods, back of Egypt. One night, in camp, they were talking about bears. Hector was the oldest hand there and they asked him, "Is there any bears around here?"

Hector said, "Yes. You just wait a few minutes, I'm gonna take the gun and I'm goin' out myself. I think I know where there's one pretty handy."

Hector took the gun. He checked and, my God, there was only one bullet. He went out anyway, only travelled for a short distance and, by God, he heard the noise. There's Mister Bear. Hector picked up the gun and let her go. The bear took a jump in the air and Hector missed. Of course, the bear was wild and he started to come after Hector.

Hector was going like hell for the camp and the bear was gaining on him. He was just about to catch him when Hector got to the door. Hector opened the door and he got in behind it. The bear slid in on the camp floor and Hector hollered, "Skin that one, boys, I'm goin' after another one!"

X584.1. Man chased by bear to camp claims that he brought it in thus since he did not want to carry it

JOSIE MACNEIL

BIG POND

204.

There was a fellow in Glace Bay who was quite witty. His name was Neil Currie. Father Al used to tease him because he was so witty.

This one day he called in to see Neil and he said, "It must be pretty tough working in the mine, coming from the farm. Going down there and it's so dark in the mine."

Neil says, "Well, Father, I work all day shifts."

J2220. Other logical absurdities

P415. Collier

205.

There were two old maids and one had to watch the other all the time because she'd wander off and they wouldn't know where she went. They had to keep their eyes on her.

This winter evening she took off. It was fine at first but later it started to storm. A terrific snowstorm, and it was cold.

The sister couldn't find her and she finally went to the glebe house and asked the priest to help. They rang the church bell and that called everybody up to the glebe house to see what was going on. The priest said, "Everybody get out and look for Maggie. She's lost."

Away they went.

The storm was getting worse and it was getting colder. Finally, one of the men saw some footprints going up the side of the mountain and thought they might have been Maggie's. Up he went and, on the other side, there was a brook. Maggie had fallen in the brook and she froze to death. This fellow managed to chop her out of the ice, threw her over his back and carried her out—and they took her to the glebe house.

When they arrived there the man said to the priest, "Well Father, if you'll have the hard time taking Maggie out of purgatory as I had taking her out of the ice, you have your work cut out."

J1260. Repartee based on church or clergy

N330. Accidental killing or death

JIM MACNEIL

BIG POND

206.

There was a man up on the mainland of Nova Scotia. Oh, he drank very heavily. He'd fall down and sleep anywhere when he got tired. It didn't matter where he was.

One night he was travelling around, drinking, and there were some people watching him. Pretty well under the weather, he headed through a cemetery and there was a grave dug that afternoon. The burial was the following day. He stumbled into the grave and he thought he was comfortable and decided to go to sleep. He was just about to doze off and one of those who'd been following him went up close and leaned over the edge of the hole.

"What are you doing in my grave?"

The man looked up and asked, "Who are you?"

He said, "I'm Paul."

"Oh, you're Paul. Well, Paul, I have a question for you."

"Yes, what is the question?"

"Paul, did you ever get a reply to all those letters to the Romans?"

J1260. Repartee based on church or clergy

J2311. Person made to believe that he is dead

X800. Humour based on drunkenness

TALE TYPES AND MOTIFS

COMPILED BY MICHAEL TAFT

TYPES

MOTIFS

ALSO AVAILABLE FROM
Breton Books

Archie Neil

THE LIFE AND STORIES OF ARCHIE NEIL CHISHOLM

by Mary Anne Ducharme

SADDLED WITH POLIO, pride, and a lack of self-discipline, Archie Neil Chisholm of Margaree Forks lived out the contradictory life of a terrific teacher floundering in alcoholism. His growth, plunge, and rise as an extraordinarily valuable person in the Cape Breton community is full of outrageous good humour and excellent storytelling.

BIOGRAPHY • ORAL HISTORY • ANTHOLOGY

PHOTOS • 248 PAGES • $18.50

Another Night

CAPE BRETON STORIES TRUE & SHORT & TALL

edited by Ronald Caplan

MORE GREAT STORYTELLING from the pages of *Cape Breton's Magazine*. Some witty, some eerie, some heart-rending, these stories convey the pleasure we take in entertaining one another.

45 STORIES • 214 PAGES • $16.25

• PRICES INCLUDE GST & POSTAGE IN CANADA •

CONTINUED ON NEXT PAGE

ALSO AVAILABLE FROM
Breton Books

Cape Breton Shipwreck Stories

1761-1955

collected & edited by Ronald Caplan

FROM THE GUT-WRENCHING TREK of the *Auguste*'s survivors to John Angus Fraser's hilarious adventures aboard the *Kismet II*, to Walter Boudreau's harrowing account of days adrift in a lifeboat while his companions died around him—a batch of good stories from Cape Breton shipwrecks, told by survivors, rescuers and passionate researchers.

From eyewitness accounts to kitchen memories, from fiction to song—these are lasting, enjoyable and often painful stories.

PHOTOS • 176 PAGES • $18.50

Cape Breton Works

MORE LIVES FROM CAPE BRETON'S MAGAZINE

edited by Ronald Caplan

THIS IS CAPE BRETON TALKING! This extraordinary mix of men's and women's lives delivers a solid dose of the courage, humour and good storytelling that make a place like Cape Breton work.

From Canada's longest-running oral history journal, these voices affirm, entertain, and inspire—and carry our stories to the world.

154 PHOTOS • 300 PAGES • $23.50

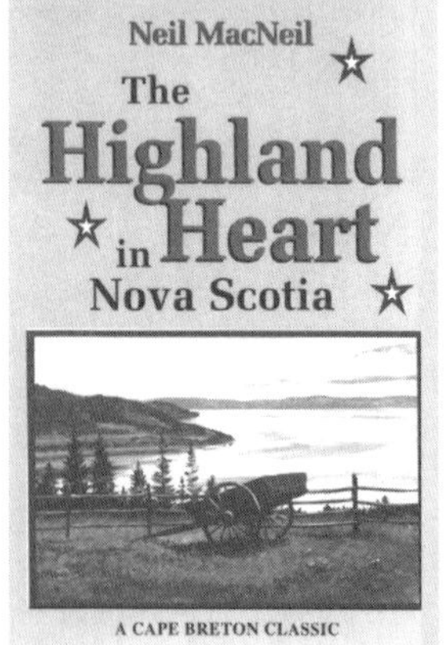

The Highland Heart in Nova Scotia

by Neil MacNeil

NEW EDITION CELEBRATES 50 YEARS of a remarkable Cape Breton Classic!

The Highland Heart in Nova Scotia is Neil MacNeil's memoir of his boyhood. This is Cape Breton pioneer history writ large, with all the purity and bravado and passion that an exiled native son brings to the world of his heart and his youth.

Wonderful writing about the peace and raw humour of Celtic Cape Breton's Golden Age, with ample doses of history and of legend.

PHOTOS • 208 PAGES • $18.50

• PRICES INCLUDE GST & POSTAGE IN CANADA •

ALSO AVAILABLE FROM
Breton Books

Father Jimmy

LIFE AND TIMES OF JIMMY TOMPKINS

by Jim Lotz and Michael R. Welton

THE ABRASIVE, COMPASSIONATE, nagging, cranky, inquisitive, generous, altogether marvelous priest from Margaree—spiritual father of the co-op movement in Nova Scotia; still its inspiration and conscience. Angered by injustice, fortified by compassion and faith, Tompkins encouraged cooperation, self-reliance and adult education to get people to make a difference in their own lives.

The roots of the worldwide Antigonish Movement—an enjoyable biography, and a tool for today.

PHOTOS • 176 PAGES • $18.50

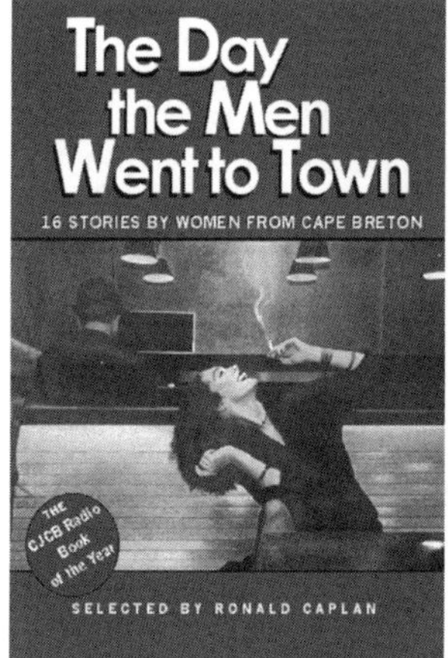

The Day the Men Went to Town

16 STORIES BY WOMEN FROM CAPE BRETON

STRONG WRITING by women who have a significant attachment to Cape Breton Island! These stories are about fisherwomen and aliens from space, the poignancy of family life and tragedy in the coal mines—and several approaches to love. Entertaining and thought-provoking.

By Lynn Coady, Joan Clark, Claudia Gahlinger, Beatrice MacNeil, Susan Zettell, Sherry D. Ramsey, Jean McNeil, Kim Williamson, Tessie Gillis, Ann-Marie MacDonald, D.C. Troicuk, Tricia Fish, Erin McNamara, Teresa O'Brien, Ellen Frith, Carol Bruneau.

176 PAGES • $18.50

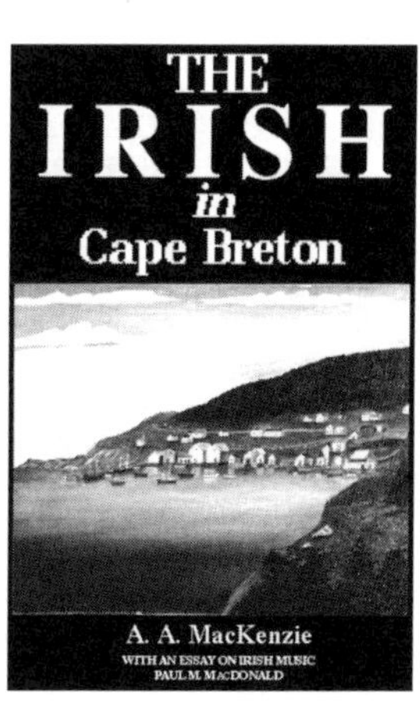

The Irish in Cape Breton

by A. A. MacKenzie

A RARE, RICH AND LIVELY history of the Irish in Cape Breton, once again showing that the recipe for authentic Cape Breton is a complex and exciting mix. MacKenzie offers here an excellent general introduction to the Irish experience and their contribution, a book stocked with details about both culture and individuals.

With an essay on Cape Breton's Irish Music by Paul M. MacDonald, and the cover painting by Bob Fitzgerald of "White Point, circa 1935."

160 PAGES • $18.50

• PRICES INCLUDE GST & POSTAGE IN CANADA •

CONTINUED ON NEXT PAGE

ALSO AVAILABLE FROM
Breton Books

The Last Gael
AND OTHER STORIES
by Ellison Robertson

SHIMMERING BETWEEN exuberant humour and almost unremitting darkness, the stories in *The Last Gael* reflect elements of life in Cape Breton, where the traditional and the urban not only coexist but engage one another, often at war in the single person or event.

Painter/author Robertson has produced a rich, satisfying book, rooted in the place and the man. These stories have plot, meaning, acute observation—and they are told with quiet, accomplished grace. This is a welcome Maritime voice

128 PAGES • $16.25

The Glace Bay Miners' Museum
—THE NOVEL
by Sheldon Currie

THE MOVIE "Margaret's Museum" has won awards in Spain, Halifax, Vancouver. And the novel behind it all is every bit as haunting and mesmerizing as the movie. Terrific storytelling with a bizarre, shattering ending, it has the guts to carry a love story set in the coal region of Cape Breton to a staggering, realistic conclusion.

PHOTOS • 130 PAGES • $18.50

The Story So Far...
11 SHORT STORIES
by Sheldon Currie

FINALLY, a collection of Currie's best stories—disturbing and compassionate. A serious book of high comedy, these stories dare to deal with our terrors and acts of tenderness, from questioning love to wanting love to actually trying to *create* love.

172 PAGES • $16.25

God & Me
by Sheila Green

18 OPEN, UNPRETENTIOUS POEMS—with 7 tender drawings by Alison R. Grapes—about family, friendship, and the heart of all religious feeling.

A gentle way of sharing wonder and relationship with a child, and a lovely keepsake for any adult

36 PAGES • $9.00

Sterling Silver
RANTS, RAVES & REVELATIONS
by Silver Donald Cameron

ESSAYS FROM OVER 25 YEARS of writing, never before in print form—*Sterling Silver* demonstrates a wide range of Silver Donald's interests.

From suicide to love and fear, craftsmanship and community—this is Silver Donald Cameron angry, hopeful, incisive and amused

232 PAGES • $21.50

Echoes from Labor's Wars
by Dawn Fraser
Industrial Cape Breton in the 1920s
Echoes of World War One
Autobiography & Other Writings
Introduction by David Frank
& Don MacGillivray

Dawn Fraser's narrative verse and stories are a powerful, compelling testament to courage, peace & community. They belong in every home, in every school.

144 PAGES • $13.00

Yankees at Louisbourg
STORY OF THE FIRST SIEGE, 1745
by George A. Rawlyk

"THE BEST AND FULLEST account of the first siege of Louisbourg," wrote historian W. S. MacNutt.

You are there for the planning and the rabble-rousing, and the day-by-day details of this critical event in Canadian history and American consciousness. "The capture of Louisbourg in 1745 was the most important military achievement of the American colonists prior to the War of the Revolution."—L. E. DEFOREST

216 PAGES • $21.50

Breton Books
Wreck Cove, Cape Breton
Nova Scotia B0C 1H0
www.capebretonbooks.com
bretonbooks@ns.sympatico.ca

SEND FOR OUR FREE CATALOGUE

CONTINUED ON NEXT PAGE